THE GIRL
FROM NOWHERE

THE GIRL FROM NOWHERE

Philip Francis Nowlan

"Creator of Buck Rogers"

WILDSIDE PRESS

THE GIRL FROM NOWHERE

Published by
Wildside Press, LLC
www.wildsidepress.com

Foreword

"Elsewhere I have set down, for whatever interest they have in this, the
25th Century, my personal recollections of the 20th Century."

This great opening literary line appeared in Philip Francis
Nowlan's 1928 classic novella "Armageddon 2419 A.D.," in
which Anthony Rogers made his classic debut. After this orig-
inal novella appeared, Anthony Rogers changed his name to
"Buck" Rogers and the rest is science-fiction history.

But, what does that have to do with "The Girl from
Nowhere"?

Well, this line is applicable to "The Girl from Nowhere,"
which has come out of fictional nowhere! Until now—more
than 65 years after this hidden treasure was originally written
—"The Girl from Nowhere" was unpublished, as it was
recently discovered in the attic of my parents' house in Bala
Cynwyd, PA, which is fittingly also the hometown of the
creation of the famous Rogers character. Science-fiction buffs
may recall that Anthony Rogers was in a 492-year "state of
suspended animation" in "Armageddon 2419 A.D.," prior to
his awakening in the 25th Century. It can likewise be said
that "The Girl from Nowhere" has been in similar suspension
for the last 65 years, and is still in good hands!

My grandfather would have taken great pride and hope

that his sole *non*-science-fiction novella, written in the 20th Century, has an equal interest in the 21st Century—certainly to his family, conceivably to his science-fiction fans, and optimistically to a new generation of young and old readers alike.

As there are similarities between the "Armageddon" storyline and the delayed discovery of "The Girl from Nowhere," it occurs to me that "The Girl from Nowhere" has withstood the test of time, much like Philip Francis Nowlan's science-fiction prophecies. On behalf of the entire Nowlan Family, we believe it has been well worth the wait!

Sally Bevlock McGovern,
Granddaughter of Philip Francis Nowlan

Introduction

Upon the Nowlan family discovery of "The Girl from Nowhere," as described in the Foreword, this novella was expected to be another science-fiction thriller by Philip Francis Nowlan, creator of Anthony "Buck" Rogers. Were we surprised! It was soon revealed that science-fiction was not his only interest—as this mystery reveals. Philip Francis Nowlan's spellbinding storytelling and affection for a strong female lead are again evidenced in this unique drama.

Set in the early part of the 20th Century, "The Girl from Nowhere" takes us on a gripping ride through criminal and legal circles in New York City. Catching the attention of Scott Duvenney, who is one of New York's leading criminal defense attorneys, the beautiful Edna Raalhof appears from nowhere. Scott Duvenney is determined to win her attention and then her affection. Treating her kindly, he cannot give the credit to his manners, but rather to his attraction. She was by no means the first woman in his life to accept or reject his advances. Because she was a tough "read", he chose to read her attitude toward him positively. Little does he know Edna Raalhof, an adventuress, seems to have an inexplicable purpose of her own, which only intrigues Scott Duvenney even more. Where did she come from? Why is she here? What are her plans? Will she discover his true dealings? Is she in cahoots with "Wildcat" Casey, a secret agent who was mystifying to both police and underworld circles - and even Scott Duvenney?

Unlike most criminal lawyers, Scott Duvenney made more money when his clients kept out of trouble than when they got in it, for he shared in the profits. Night life in the city police station was rarely exciting, and Scott's clients always seemed to be devising plans to foil the city force. Later realizing Edna's true intentions, Scott would soon discover that they had somewhat convergent interests. Caught between two fires, threatened on one side by a girl, and on the other by Wildcat Casey whose methods were often disconcerting, Scott Duvenney felt the menace of unseen powers closing in around him.

The above brief abstract of "The Girl from Nowhere" depicts the versatility of Philip Francis Nowlan. For an author known for his science-fiction, this mystery depicts another of his passions. In fact, early in Nowlan's writing career, he wrote syndicated columns for publication, such as "Harvey Hunt, Detective" which featured a mystery in one episode and gave the solution in the next. While it will remain a "mystery" why he did not focus more on writing mysteries, one thing is clear: Whenever Philip Francis Nowlan stared into the flickering flames of his fireplace, his children knew to leave him alone because inside his keen mind, there was a genius at work.

Brett McGovern,
Grandson-in-Law of Philip Francis Nowlan

Chapter 1

The Shadow Car

Scott Duvenney gazed at the girl in baffled irritation. It was a new experience for him to find a woman whom he could attract, yet not dominate.

She flipped her cigarette into a clump of bushes and slid lightly from the railing.

"I have the next two dances taken, Scott," she said. "That leaves only the last. We can discuss this further then—my dear." Before he could reply she had stepped from his side to meet the clean cut, muscular youngster who had come to claim his dance.

Duvenney bowed and managed a smile as they turned away. But the smile quickly gave place to a scowl. He could have understood it all if he had—but no, it had been marriage that he offered her. An adventuress, living by her wits and none too scrupulous in her use of them, she had as much as admitted it to him. Yet she had seemed genuinely displeased at his proposal. He could not understand. He had the wealth to satisfy her every whim. Already one of New York's leading criminal lawyers, his power was growing. Perhaps it was his reputation to which she objected. But who was she to flout him on that account?

Edna Raalhof and her father had appeared from nowhere. Their only visible circle of acquaintances was recently acquired at the club, through Duvenney's own introduction, and nobody realized better than Duvenney himself that this was but a questionable recommendation. It was indeed, together with the vague generalities she vouchsafed concerning her past, sufficient to make her the subject of many a whispered conversation.

Needless to say, her daring toilettes, the apparent lack of consciousness with which she wore them, the almost boyish directness of speech which seemed normal to her, the occasional half revelation of a sophistication far beyond her years and contrasting oddly with her youthful vitality of face and figure, all served to intensify the attention she attracted and the reserve with which she was received, particularly by those of her own sex.

Duvenney had not bothered before to ferret out her motives in encouraging him. It was enough for him that she had done so. He cared little whether she was attracted by himself or his money, so long as he obtained her. Until now, he had never doubted that he would.

Then, after deliberately leading him on, she had calmly waved him aside. His anger surged at the memory of the callous little laugh with which she had done so. Viciously he chewed his cigar until it fell apart between his teeth and spat it out with disgust.

The incident broke the spell of his thoughts, and he realized for the first time that he was being paged by one of the club attendants.

"Here," he called. "What is it?"

"Telephone, sir," was the reply.

Duvenney stepped inside and threaded his way across the dance floor in the direction of the booths.

"That you, Mr. Duvenney?" came the voice over the wire. "This is Cranweiler talking. Greasy Gorman and Solly Wertheimer's just been pinched."

"Well, what of it? I'll go see them tomorrow. What's the idea of bothering me with it tonight? Call me up at the office in the morning."

"Sure I'll call up in the morning, if you say so, but I just thought you'd like to know that Wildcat Casey's in town."

Duvenney started.

"What's that?" he snapped.

"I say Wildcat Casey's at work in New York. At least it looks like it was him that Greasy and Solly collided with. I got it from a loose mouthed cop over here in Brooklyn that they were picked up here this evening. It seems like some flatfoot, making his rounds, pokes open the door of a private garage that ought to be locked, and finds them bound and gagged, and beat up fierce, lying in a machine that's been stolen from some guy up in the Bronx. You know, the one you—"

"Shut up, you bonehead," warned Duvenney angrily. "Remember you're talking over a telephone. Save it until tomorrow morning. And come to the office; don't telephone." And without waiting for Cranweiler's reply, Duvenney slammed up the receiver.

Thoughtfully he made his way to the porch again and sought a chair in a deserted corner. This business was serious.

Patrick F., otherwise "Wildcat," Casey was a factor to be reckoned with, a mystery in both police and underworld circles, a secret agent whose clients even were seldom known and who never revealed his identity. It was a question indeed, whether more than a very select few of these clients had ever come in personal contact with him.

Duvenney might or might not be able to extricate his two "clients" from the clutches of the law, but the stolen machine would be returned to its owner. And it would be a long time before Greasy and Solly would recover sufficiently to resume successful operations. Their nerves would be broken worse than their bodies.

Criminals who had had the misfortune to mix it up with Casey all testified that there was something terrifying in the smashing, tearing attack of the "Wildcat" that broke their nerves in much the same manner that wrecks those of railroad engineers.

Duvenney was concerned. Unlike most criminal lawyers, he made more money when his clients kept out of trouble than when they got in it, for he shared in their profits, which were secured largely through his counsel and direction, as well as under the cloak of political protection which he was able to throw over them.

It was typical of the man's supreme confidence that he did not for a moment fear that he himself would fall into any net, which Casey might spread. He was simply irritated that his operations should be interfered with and his profits temporarily cut down.

First it was the girl that balked him. Then this fellow

Casey had to butt in. He swore aloud. Just why, he asked himself, had she treated him that way, and why should he allow himself to be upset by it? Edna Raalhof was by no means the first woman in his life—neither the first to accept nor to reject his advances. Could it be that he was actually falling in love with the girl? He must get a grip on himself. This would never do. With an effort he shook off the thought and arose, almost colliding, in his preoccupation, with a figure, which had just emerged from the dance hall.

"Hello there, Burrell," he said, "I didn't hear you coming."

"Rubber soles," explained Burrell, mopping his brow, "Always wear 'em to dances. You look worried, old man. Bad business. Unnatural for a lawyer to worry, you know. Better come and have a smile with me. Max has just got in some new stuff that tastes like old times. Come along, I want your opinion on it."

"Pretty good stuff," remarked Duvenney. "Where'd you get it, Max?" he asked.

"Couldn't say, sir," replied the barkeeper. "Mr. Wilson got it for us, but he didn't say where. Brought it out in the car tonight."

"He gets it from a couple of fellows named Gorman and Wertheimer," explained Burrell, "who have tapped an old stock somewhere, he says. I think I'll have to get him to put me in touch with them. Have another won't you?"

"No thanks," said the lawyer hastily. "This is the last dance, I think, and I have it booked. See you later, Ted." And as he turned toward the dance hall, he was unaware of a twinkle, ever so faint, in the steady gaze of the latter.

The dance, however, was already underway, and as he stood in the doorway he saw Edna at the other end of the hall, again in the arms of the youth who had taken her from him earlier in the evening. She had wasted no time in waiting for him apparently, and he had missed his tete a tete.

He had missed more, had he only known it; a telephone call which she had made to the same pay station in the city from which Cranweiler had called him, a call in which she had received virtually the same information that Cranweiler had given him.

As he stood there, waiting for a chance to catch her glance, he gradually became aware that the girl was subtly avoiding his end of the hall. As she emerged from the dressing room, just as the last strain of the good-night waltz was dying away, she found him waiting for her.

"May I run you home Edna?" he asked. "I think you owe me that permission at least, after robbing me of that promised dance the way you did."

"Now that's awfully sweet of you, Scott," she laughed, "and really my dear, I'd love to go with you, but tonight it is your fate always to be a little bit late. I have just accepted Mildred Malason's invitation to go with them in their new Colwyn sedan, but if you yearn terribly to take me for a ride I have no engagement for tomorrow evening and —"

"It's a deal then," said Duvenney quickly. "At what time shall I call?"

"Come for dinner," she said. "Father and I always dine at seven. And," she added softly with a quick glance around, "father is not dining home tomorrow." And with a little laugh she ran down the steps toward the waiting machine.

With regained complacency, Duvenney sought his own car. Perhaps she had only been teasing him after all. She had refused him. But she had also invited him to dine with her, alone. He chose to read her attitude toward him in the invitation rather than in the refusal.

But he paused, startled, with one foot on the running board. What was it Cranweiler had told him the day before about a plan of "the boys" to stage a hold-up on the Old Hickory Road? Why, this was the road the Malasons would be taking to reach Edna's cottage!

Suppose—.

He leaped quickly into the machine. Dick Malason, the youngster with whom she had been dancing, was a hot-head. There might be a shooting. He would have to stop that at all costs. If he could just manage to beat the Malason machine to that lonely stretch of road by a substantial margin, he might substitute himself as the victim, then, when the bandits recognize him, call the hold-up off. Or, if the Malason machine came up too quickly, he might pretend to scare them off.

The engine whirred in response to the touch of his toe on the starter, and the big car lurched forward silently as he rapidly shifted the gears. Through the gates and into the road he swung, and the whir of the engine rose to a hissing moan as the long strip of road illumined by his headlights began to rush toward him.

The Malasons must be a mile ahead of him, he figured, and he had about six miles in which to catch and pass them. If only that young fool, Dick Malason, would allow him to pass without attempting to race or block him, all would be well.

So intently was Duvenney watching for the faint red tail lamp of the machine somewhere ahead that he never glanced over his shoulder. Had he done so he would have noticed two dull headlights which apparently floated after him through the night without effort, the eyes of a silent shadow car which easily pulled closer to him on the hills and curves, to sink back a bit at spots where the road straightened out.

Chapter 2

The Hold Up

Edna Raalhof was quite aware of the attention she had been attracting among the members of the Penton Country Club. She did not deceive herself as to its nature. In fact, she had expected it, and in a sense played for it. Had she been able to contrive an introduction for her father and herself through some other member than Duvenney, it would have been different. But she hadn't.

Edna's finesse lay largely in her readiness to seize an opportunity and her ability to work with whatever tools might be at hand. But her intuition was by no means confined to problems of the present. The girl had an almost uncanny prescience, and when she chose, she could reach her objectives by long, circuitous routes. Just at present her immediate purpose was to achieve a position among the frequenters of the Penton Club superior to and independent of that held by Duvenney.

In the Malasons, mother and daughter, she had long before sensed an aversion of gossip and an independence of others' opinions. So Mildred's invitation had come to her as an opportunity, an indication of a sincerely cordial attitude and one decidedly to be capitalized.

"It was good of you to ask me, Mrs. Malason," she murmured, "And it's going to take you out of your way too."

"I fancy that several of the men thought it was very horrid of us, my dear," laughed Mrs. Malason. "I don't think Mr. Duvenney thanked us a bit. Do you know him very well?"

"He introduced us at the club. Dad met him in a political way," Edna said adroitly, and added, "I hate politics."

"Don't blame you for not liking the kind he indulges in—Duvenney I mean, of course," drawled Dick Malason as with a dextrous twist he steered the sedan around a bad spot in the road.

"Why Dick," chided Mildred, "one would think you were jealous."

"I am," he said, risking a glance and a grin over his shoulder at Edna; then, noting Edna's faint smile, "But I'm more jealous of this fellow Burrell. Nobody seems to know exactly who he is or where he came from. I wish you'd vamp his past out of him, Mil. I'm quite sure there's something about him that Miss Raalhof should be protected from."

"I'm game," murmured Mildred dreamily from the depths of the rear seat. "There's something so deliciously romantic about him, especially when he's sitting in the telephone booth just behind Mr. Duvenney, with the receiver to his ear—and his finger on the hook."

"What?" exclaimed Dick.

"Why, Mildred!" exclaimed her mother.

"How strange!" said Edna, sitting up suddenly.

"And where were you to see all this?" asked Dick.

"In the booth behind Mr. Burrell," said Mildred softly.

"With your finger also on the hook?"

"No, Angel Face. If you must know, I was clandestinely phoning to one of my lovers, and it's none of your business which one. Only I hope he wasn't making an engagement with himself for me, for I confess I was so interested in the post of Mr. Burrell's finger that I wasn't paying much attention to what he was saying."

"You must have been mistaken, Mildred," said Mrs. Malason.

"But Mamma, I wasn't. I tell you I saw it. I was so close I could have touched him except for the glass partition."

"Hush, Mildred," admonished her mother, "or Miss Raalhof will think you're taking Dick's suggestion for her protection seriously."

"Or that she's trying to block his efforts and stimulate my interest in Mr. Burrell," smiled Edna. "I adore plots and everything. You didn't overhear what Mr. Duvenney was saying that he was so interested in, did you, Mildred?"

"Just a snatch," said Mildred, "when Mr. Duvenney got excited. He said 'Shut up you bonehead!' just like that, and added something about seeing him at the office in the morning, and not telephoning. Then he got mad and slammed up the receiver, and Mr. Burrell hung up his receiver and relieved his finger, and I went on talking to Reed—I mean to the person I was—"

"Reed Mason!" exclaimed Dick triumphantly. "I suspected it. Mother, our little Mildred must be getting serious when—"

"Don't be silly, Dick," Mildred cut in with a confusion,

"Oh, you make me sick!"

And at that moment Edna won a valuable friend by the unobserved and sympathetic little squeeze she gave Mildred's arm.

Chuckling to himself, Dick swung the machine to the left. They had left the State Road now, and were swaying gently down the Old Hickory Road with that motion that is only to be experienced when a heavy car travels a dirt road in smooth condition.

For the most part, the road ran through a forest, which the brilliant headlights of the Colwyn revealed as a silvery tunnel for long stretches where the foliage almost met overhead . . .

It was in the middle of one of these stretches, after rounding an easy curve that Dick jammed on his brakes and brought the car to a screeching stop. A few feet ahead was a touring car, apparently abandoned, and standing diagonally across the road in such fashion as to block it effectually.

A thrill of apprehension swept over Dick Malason. In a flash, his mind summed up the situation: the loneliness of the road, his single-handed responsibility for the three women, and the fact that he had no weapon. For a moment he sat as though paralyzed. Then the spell was broken by Mildred's voice.

"Well, of all things!"

"Now who do you suppose could have left a car like that?" ventured Mrs. Malason, then hesitatingly, "Do you think—"

"What difference does it make?" said Dick, fumbling a

bit nervously in a convenient side-pocket for a heavy monkey-wrench and at the same time getting out of the machine. "It's a cinch we can't get by unless we move it. I'll slide it around on the side of the road."

"You'll have to push it, Mr. Malason, " said Edna, "I'll help you. Really, I'm awfully strong." And she jumped lightly to the ground.

Dick, whose glance had been roving uneasily up and down both sides of the road, was beginning to feel reassured. Nothing moved, nor did any sound come from the trees except the hum of insect life.

"Oh, I can manage it all right, Miss Raalhof. See, there's a slope to the road. You'll get those slippers of yours all dusty and your hands dirty. Here, I'll show you how easy it is." He turned and walked quickly toward the touring car, reaching in to release the brake. Then, he stood galvanized as a voice came from the woods.

"Stick 'em up, bo! I got you covered. An' drop that wrench. Now keep yer hands up and git over there to the other side of the road facin' the woods. Quick, now. We got no time to waste."

At the same moment another voice spoke from the woods a few feet from the sedan.

"You Janes git outa that car—and you in the road there you just stand right where y'are, see. Now you other two skirts line up right alongside her, see."

It was over very quickly. The bandit nearest the sedan stepped out of the woods and crossed over to the three women. Mildred, white and trembling, stared in wild-eyed fright. Her mother gasped, speechless in futile indignation. The fellow winced a bit at the glare of suppressed fury in Edna's eyes. But all three had to give up their valuables. From Mildred and her mother particularly, he got a small fortune in rings and a diamond pendant.

Once Dick tensed himself to whirl and spring to their aid, but the thug who was guarding him sensed it, and his sharp warning brought the youth back to a sense of his utter helplessness.

Then the bandits lined them all up across the road, facing back in the direction from which they had come, backed their own machine around to clear the road, ran the sedan past it, and with a start of some thirty yards on their victims, drove off with both cars.

"It's five miles to anywhere," finally ventured Dick, addressing the blackness around him, "and we can't even see the road. I—I'm a hell of a hero, I am," he finished ruefully.

Edna Raalhof laughed. "You're a live one anyhow," she said. "If you had tried to do anything foolish, you might not be."

"I think there's a machine coming," said Mildred tremulously. The faint gleam of approaching headlights lit up the trees at one side of the road.

A moment later, Scott Duvenney's car swung around the curve and came to a stop as he saw them standing in the road . . . A quick glance told him all were there and none seemed to be hurt, and it was a feeling of relief that he hid beneath a simulated astonishment as he jumped out of his car and ran toward them.

"We've been held up," volunteered Dick.

"The devil you say!" ejaculated the lawyer, "And they got your car too, didn't they? You're not hurt, are you, Edna?" He turned toward the girl with solicitude.

"No," she said in level tones, glancing at him keenly, for she had sensed, as the others had not, a false note in his expression of surprise. "And neither are Mrs. Malason, nor Miss Malason, nor Mr. Malason—fortunately."

"Confound it all," said Duvenney, "I wish I had been a little closer behind you folks. I would—"

"Yes, it is too bad, isn't it?" continued the girl in the same level tone. "Still, I think we're lucky you came along at all. We never would have looked for you to be going home by way of the Old Hickory Road. It makes quite a long detour when one is going back to the city, and especially at this time of night."

This was an angle of the adventure that Duvenney had not thought of. As a matter of fact, branching off on the Old Hickory Road lengthened the trip back to the city from some twelve miles to about twenty-seven. Not knowing his real interest in that hold up, what would the Malasons think? Were Edna's words dictated by suspicion that he knew the affair was planned, or was she merely warning him covertly to forestall any suspicion on the part of the Malasons that he might have been going to her little cottage at Clover Hill?

"Why—er—the fact is—I'm spending the weekend with friends over in South Hills," he said, naming a spot some twenty miles beyond Clover Hill.

"Oh," exclaimed Mildred weakly. She and Dick had glanced quickly at each other. In the minds of both there flashed the memory of Duvenney's telephone conversation and the appointment he had made for the next morning at his office.

"I'm afraid we'll have to trespass on your kindness to take us home Mr. Duvenney," said Mrs. Malason.

"Why, of course, of course," said the lawyer. "Forgive me for keeping you standing here, ladies. It will be a rather tight squeeze for all of us, but we can manage it. Let's see. I'll see you folks home first, then I can drop Miss Raalhof on my way back to South Hills."

"I think," said Mrs. Malason, "that we better see Miss Raalhof home first."

"If you don't mind," added Edna sweetly.

"Certainly. Of course. That would be much better," hurriedly acquiesced Duvenney, "I didn't think. This occurrence—yes—that will be the much better plan."

As Duvenney's car pulled away from the scene of the hold-up, Mildred Malason relaxed suddenly, leaning limply against Edna.

"Did you see it?" she whispered.

"See what, dear?" Edna asked.

"The other machine. There was a car in back of Mr. Duvenney, Edna. I just caught a glimpse of its dimmed lights through the trees around that curve in the road. It must have stopped. I was so scared. I had a feeling that somebody was creeping up on us."

"What's that, Miss Malason?" asked Duvenney, who caught the girl's words. He glanced quickly over his shoulder. He saw the section of the road where the hold-up had occurred illumined by the spotlight of a standing car, and the silhouetted figure of a man who seemed to be searching for something on the ground. Smothering a curse, Duvenney stepped hard on the accelerator. Into his mind too, there now flashed the memory of Cranweiler's phone message, and the name of "Wildcat" Casey.

Chapter 3

Casey Scares Again

Precariously balancing himself on one chair and his feet on another, Trooper MacNeill slept uneasily and noisily. At the desk, Sergeant Rafferty conned a well-thumbed joke book with perfunctory interest. He had read all those jokes before. More than that, he knew a lot of better ones. Still he read. There was nothing else to do.

Night life in a city police station is rarely exciting, and even less interesting in the village headquarters of a unit of the State Police motorcycle squad. So when the telephone call came, Rafferty rather welcomed it, in a desultory sort of way.

"Yeah?" he queried, putting the receiver to his ear.

"State Police?" asked the concise voice at the other end of the wire.

"Yeah," said Rafferty again, but in the tone of voice which signifies acquiescence rather than interrogation.

"Want to nail a couple of stick-up men?"

"Yeah," repeated Rafferty, this time registering alertness, at the same time reaching for pencil and pad.

"They pulled the job on Old Hickory Road, two miles east of State Road. Held up the machine of John T. Malason, robbed young Malason, his sister and mother and a girlfriend, took the Malason's car and their own and went East with it. The Malason car is a Colwyn Six sedan, 1923 model. The bandit car is a Beckwith Touring, 1922, two new Berson cord tires on rear, Goodwell cord, half worn, on left front wheel. Blackstone grid-tread fabric on the right. If you—"

"Did'ja see this stick-up?" snapped Rafferty suspiciously.

"No, but—"

"Well, how'd'ya know so much about this bandit car?"

"My name's Casey," patiently explained the voice, "Patrick J. Casey. Perhaps that makes it a little clearer and—"

"Oh, yeah." This time Rafferty managed to inject quick understanding with something of apology into the word.

"That's a dirt road, you know, fairly soft. It was easy to tell the make and condition of the tires from the marks the treads made. The bandits had backed their car across the road, so I was able to measure the wheelbase. That together with the size of the wheels—I measured the distance between two marks of the same gash in one of the tires and calculated the diameter—makes it certain it was a Beckwith 1922, and I overheard young Malason say it was a touring car."

"Some memory you got, Mr. Casey."

"Memory nothing. I just carry what you fellows ought to have sense enough to carry, a notebook with the specifications of the different makes and models in it.

"Now listen. Here's a tip for you I think will work out. In getting to the scene of the hold-up, that bandit car must have come over a stretch of road that's been freshly tarred. Some of the tar and pebbles dripped off the under side of the mudguards while it was standing there. There's a good chance they'll go back the same way they came. If you work quick you may getta couple of your men to head them off. Do you know of any road around here that's been freshly tarred?"

"Not offhand. But I guess I can get it from some of the boys. Where you telephoning from, Mr. Casey?"

"No place where anybody could give you a description of me," laughed Casey. "By the way, this thing happened about twenty or twenty-five minutes ago."

"All right, sir," Rafferty said. "We'll do our best to land 'em, Mr. Casey. Thanks for the tip."

"That bird's some quick worker," whispered Rafferty as he hung up. "Hey, MacNeill, snap out of it. Where's there any fresh tar on the roads East, North or South of the Old Hickory Road at a point two miles East of State Road?"

"Ugh?" grunted MacNeill, starting up and barely avoiding disaster to his balance on the two chairs. "Come again."

He scratched his head sleepily and considered, as Rafferty repeated the question. "Why—er—there's a stretch just been tarred down there on Mill Run Pike about half way between Old Hickory Road and City Line. Quite sure that's the only one around this section of the country."

"Umm," Rafferty calculated slowly, "That'd be about thirteen miles down Old Hickory and four miles down Mill Run, seventeen altogether. Say, Weiss ought to catch 'em coming down Mill Run. He's got Loman with 'im. And I could swing Dains and Weller over to close in on 'em from behind."

Three minutes later two farmers, at widely separated

points, had been roused by Rafferty's phone, and had snapped on red signal lights on their porches. Not more than six minutes more had passed before police motorcycles had roared up to the doors of these two farmers and four State troopers had received their orders.

The rest was easy. An hour later two troopers drove up to headquarters, in a Colwyn sedan and a Beckwith touring car, each with a handcuffed prisoner who had been "caught with the goods."

It had been Duvenney's intention, as he drew up at the gate before the little cottage, which Edna and her father were occupying for the summer, to tell her that he must return and have a talk with her after taking the Malasons home. Dick Malason spoiled his plan, however, when he leaped quickly from the machine and held out his hand to Edna.

"I'll see you to the door, Miss Raalhof," he offered. Then, as they went up the walk . . .

"You must think me awfully yellow to have stood there and let those roughnecks put it over us like that."

"Why, I think you did the sensible, manly thing," replied Edna. "You were unarmed, and there's no telling what would have happened to your mother and sister if you had angered them."

"I was thinking of you too, Miss Raalhof," he said, and Edna, in the shelter of the darkness, smiled, then winced a bit at the half shy intimation in the youngster's tone. It came home to her with a little shock that she was ages older than he, yet she was only twenty-two, and he was hardly less than that.

"You'll have to prove you don't think badly of me," he

was saying. "There's a dance at the club Thursday night. May I take you?"

Edna paused, her key in the lock. The opportunity fitted splendidly into her plans to cultivate the Malasons. Yet she did not seize it. For an instant she wavered. Then, in a low voice, as though afraid she might change her mind, she said, "I'm sorry, Mr. Malason. I have an engagement. But, thank you so much for your kindness in seeing me home."

Inside the door she paused, listening for the roar of Duvenney's cut-out. Then, she threw off her wrap with a sigh.

"Miss Raalhof," she remarked to herself in imitation of Dick's respectful tones, "You're a fool. You haven't got sense enough to take—to take—candy from a child."

"What did you say, Edna?" asked her father indistinctly from the room beyond, where he sat perusing a copy of a theatrical magazine, with a highball within easy reach.

"Oh, are you up still? I was just talking to myself again," she said flippantly, entering the room and throwing herself into an easy chair.

Sigmund Raalhof was nothing if not consistent. Nature had endowed him in high degree with the faculty of impersonation, a faculty which in his younger days he had put to many and varied uses; none of them, however, behind the footlights. In those days, he had been known to his intimates as Samuel Raalhof. It had been about ten years since he adopted the name of Sigmund, upon the realization of certain budding capabilities in his daughter, and of the necessity for providing them with a natural, social protective-coloring. So, he became a middle-aged cosmopolitan, impeccable in dress and manner, with slightly sporting proclivities and a suspicion of foreign precision in his speech. He never overdid his part, but for ten years he had been living it, until it had become second nature to him. He had even cultivated casual and friendly intimacy with a considerable number of stage beauties during that period, though previously he had had no inclination in that direction.

He laid down his magazine and removed his black ribboned glasses, looking at Edna with eyes slightly bleary.

"Well?" he asked gently, reaching for his highball.

"I've had a new experience. The Malasons were bringing me home and we were held up."

"Held up?" he blinked uncomprehendingly.

"Yes," she replied, irritated by his dullness, "Held up. Stuck up. Waylaid by auto bandits. Robbed, if you get what I mean."

With a grunt of only mild surprise, he reached again for his glass. "Did you not have with you your automatic?" he asked.

"Oh, you're impossible tonight, father!" she exclaimed. "If you don't let that stuff alone, you're going to pull a bone-head play someday. You don't suppose I'd leave my cloak with a gun in it in the hands of a club attendant, do you? And if you see any place in this gown where I could conceal it, I wish you'd tell me." She raised her arms the better to reveal the tightness with which the soft folds of silk clung to her slender form. "Besides, would I let the Malasons know I was in the habit of carrying deadly weapons?"

"You are indeed a beautiful girl, Edna," he reflected irrelevantly. "With your vivacity, with your figure, you could marry a multi-millionaire and place us both beyond the reach of want for the rest of our lives. But there, that always annoys you. We will let it pass. Let us talk rather of Duvenney, and this wild scheme of yours to—"

"We will not," Edna said flatly. "I won't discuss it any further than to tell you that Duvenney and I are dining here alone tomorrow evening. You may go in town if you choose, or remain here in hiding as a protection to your darling daughter. I don't care. And things are breaking our way. I've got that man Cranweiler under my thumb at last, and he told me today that Wildcat Casey is at work on the auto thefts in this section. Duvenney is getting nervous over it. That will make him easier to handle."

"I had better not interfere with your handling of him, my dear," said Raalhof. "I will go in town."

"Good," said Edna. "Then you won't be able to spoil anything." And with a glance of scorn, she left the room.

Raalhof proceeded to mix another highball.

Edna undressed slowly. Her mind was preoccupied with the events of the evening. Why had Burrell been eavesdropping on Duvenney's telephone conversation at the club? Who was Burrell? To whom had Duvenney been talking? Was it to Ed Cranweiler? The latter had told her he intended to call the lawyer at the club and tell him of Casey's entrance into the situation. Why had Duvenney followed the Malason machine over Old Hickory Road? She did not believe his rather lame explanation of a weekend trip to South Hills. Were those bandits "clients" of his, and had he been apprised of their plans?

Was he trying to get to the scene in time to prevent the hold up, or to strike a pose as a rescuer?

And above all, who had followed him that third car, and what had he been doing there after they drove away? Was it Wildcat Casey? Was it Burrell? Was Burrell Casey?

Edna sat on the edge of her bed for a long time, lost in thought, her eyes fixed unseeingly on the soft glow of the rose-shaded lamp. In the deep silence, she became suddenly aware of the ticking of the little china clock on her boudoir table. Her glance shifted quickly to it. Ten minutes past three. A plan was forming in her mind. Yes, there would be time.

Swiftly, she arose and went to the carved chest at the far end of the room. Unlocking it, she took therefrom a complete outfit of man's clothing. Beneath them her slim figure would require nothing but a brassiere to conceal its femininity. She dressed quickly but carefully. Sighing over the passage of the vogue for bobbed hair, which had required nothing but a cap to conceal it if one had it cut properly, she pinned her tresses close to her head and adjusted over them a marvelously fitting wig.

The image which she inspected in her mirror with some satisfaction was that of a slender, clean cut youth in a neatly pressed suit of dark blue. A dark check cap completed the make-up.

Edna slipped lightly downstairs. The light was out in her father's study, but she needed none to tell her where to find an electric flashlight and an automatic. She opened the back door softly and made her way silently down to the garage.

The night was dark. The well-oiled doors of the garage

gave forth no squeak, and had the Raalhof's nearest neighbors been gazing from their windows at this hour they could not have noticed the shadow of the long, low roadster as it purred its way softly through the maze of trees without a light.

Chapter 4

Trapped

Not until Edna had put more than a half mile between herself and the cottage did she snap on the lights, nor put on greater speed than her machine could make in silence. Then, keeping the speedometer dial in the neighborhood of thirty miles an hour, she settled back for the long drive into the city.

She could not rest now until she had determined whether or not Ted Burrell was what he seemed, or if his identity was but a cloak assumed by Wildcat Casey. That it was a dangerous adventure to burglarize the apartment of a man whose very name was a terror to professional criminals she knew full well, and in this knowledge, her nervous and mental tension rose to a high pitch. In her state of alert exhilaration, it required all her will power to hold her machine down to the speed she had selected as safe. It would not do to be arrested for speeding in her present disguise.

Mentally, she estimated the chances of her adventure. If Burrell was merely Burrell, she had little to fear. Even if he should catch her in the act of rifling his papers, she had no doubt of her ability either to outwit or handle him. But, if Burrell were Casey—well, at least he would be totally unprepared for her move. Of all men in the world, Casey should be the least likely to expect a burglar would give him anything but a wide birth. As she drove, Edna worked out the details of her plan.

Burrell, she knew, lived in a small apartment house in a quiet residential section of the city. If she remembered rightly it was one of those exclusive houses boasting an automatic elevator but no night attendant at the door. It would have a back entrance, no doubt.

Edna drove slowly past the place, but did not stop. Instead, she swung her machine around the corner, pulling up to the curb at a spot where the parked car would not be likely to attract attention. The spot she selected was about equidistant from two residences and close to the alley into which the back door of the apartment house should open. There were lights in both the residences, even at this hour. It would look as though the owner of the machine were visiting in either one or the other of them.

She shut off the motor, and glancing quickly up and down the deserted street, slipped out and walked rapidly around the corner.

Inside the door of the apartment house she hesitated before the row of letter boxes and telephones. She had hoped to avoid speaking to anyone, for fear that her voice would betray her disguise. But, there was no one about, and it would be wise to make sure that Burrell was not at home before breaking in. So she took down the receiver of his telephone and pressed the button. If he answered she could ask for some fictitious name. If not, she would proceed with her plan.

Several rings failed to bring any response, so Edna determined to act. First she slipped back through the main hall, locating the door which led into a sort of storeroom, at the other end of which, she rightly conjectured, she would find the door leading into the alley.

This door she opened cautiously, slipping the latch before she closed it again. Then, with the aid of her pocket flash she familiarized herself with the storeroom until she was sure she would be able to find her way through it quickly in the dark if need be.

Having thus prepared for her retreat, she went back into the main hall again, and after making sure that nobody was around, entered the elevator and ran it to Burrell's floor. Since the door at the end of the public hall on this floor gave access to the fire escape, she selected a window opening on the latter as the easiest means of access to Burrell's rooms.

This window, she found, was not locked, and with a little sigh of satisfaction she slipped back into her pocket the slender steel blade with which she had intended forcing it. Raising the window softly she swung herself quickly over the sill and slipped to one side, standing with bated breath. But no sound except her own restrained breathing and the indeterminate night sounds of the city reached her straining ears. She flashed on her torch for an instant.

The room in which she stood was evidently the one Burrell used as a living room. In the one brief flash she noted the desk at her side, near the window, the easy chair, table and reading lamp opposite, and at the left the door leading obviously to the bedroom. On the right was a short passageway leading to the door of the apartment . . .

If any evidence existed in the apartment that Burrell was Casey, undoubtedly she would find it in the desk.

One final glance at the arrangement of doors and windows, and she had formed her plan of retreat if she were interrupted. At the first sound of key in lock she would slip over the windowsill. From that point, she had the alternative of stepping into the main hall from the fire escape after Burrell had entered his rooms, or if there were others in the hall she could go down the fire escape and drop into the alley.

Not caring to risk the electric lights, Edna snapped on her flashlight again, and laid it on the desk while she made a diligent search. Systematically, she went through the few bills and letters, all in the name of Mr. Theodore Burrell. In none of them did she find any clue to an identity other than the man professed.

Unconsciously, she pictured him to herself, as she went through his papers, as she had known him at the Penton Country Club. Always faultlessly and even expensively attired, usually in a sports suit, his manner was that of a man whose life had progressed along sheltered and cultured paths. He bore himself as one accustomed to move in the highest social circles, yet he had not impressed Edna as a "society man." He could be at home among these people, yet Edna sensed that he was not one of them. There was no air of superiority about him, nor yet of forced democracy. In his keen grey eyes, there was no sign of self-indulgence nor flaccid life. But neither had he the air of the preoccupied and busy man of affairs, neither the nervousness nor the relaxation of the man whose brain is keyed up all day to business or professional problems. He could turn a compliment neatly, hold his own in the polite banter of good fellowship, or converse seriously on any topic. On the whole, he was conspicuous neither for shortcomings nor unusual capabilities in any direction, so far as a casual observer might note. At the club he was accepted as a matter of course, and it never seemed to occur to anybody that nobody knew anything much about him, except that he had been introduced and elected to membership by the committee several weeks previously.

Edna Raalhof found it difficult to think of him in the role of a detective, a man sufficiently schooled in the ways of crime, or sufficiently associated with criminals to be a successful thief hunter. And as this thought flashed through her mind, she became conscious of a vague shame, such as she had felt when Dick Malason left her at the door of her cottage. The feeling irritated her.

As her brain grasped the import of the letter, which she now held in her hand, however, this half conscious train of thought was swept out of her mind. The letter was addressed, like the others to Theodore Burrell. It was the context which caught her attention.

"Dear Ted," it ran, in a well simulated friendly tone, "I fully appreciate your reasons for playing a lone hand in that little game of yours, but really I think you underestimate the advantages of specialized assistance. Two heads may not be better than one, but ten eyes can see more than two, and ten ears hear more. I'm not inclined to be impatient, but the bird you're stalking is a wary one, and you admit yourself it is no easy task to climb up his nest without his spotting you. I can find you several assistants who are impervious to threats or money, and who would feel honored to work under your direction. I can't very well catalog my talents here, since it is your desire to keep this whole matter on such a confidential basis, but if you'll just say the word I'll put you in touch with them."

The letter was signed "Charley." Edna scrutinized the envelope. It was postmarked Chicago, but like the letterhead, it was perfectly plain.

Edna no longer had any doubt. By itself the letter might have meant nothing to her. But there was also to be considered the fact that Burrell had appeared but recently, that Wildcat Casey was at work on the automobile thefts of the ring in which Duvenney was the guiding and guarding genius, that Burrell had been eavesdropping on Duvenney, that he had been at the country club that night, and might well have been the driver of the shadow car which had followed Duvenney to the scene of the hold-up. The evidence was only circumstantial. But Edna was not burdened with the limitations which the law places on courts and juries. She no longer doubted. Burrell was Casey. And she was probably the only person aside from the writer of this who knew it. Burrell suffered in her estimation as a result of her discovery, but at the moment she was thinking rather of the powerful weapon which the knowledge placed in her hands.

At this juncture, she sat up with a start. Her ear caught a faint squeaking sound. For the fraction of a second a paralyzing thrill shot through her. The sound had not come from the quarter from which she was prepared to receive her

warning. It had come from the bedroom, which she had thought empty.

But only for the smallest fraction of a second did the girl hesitate. Her hand shot out to grasp the flashlight and snap it off. The sound she had heard was that of bedsprings. Her imagination saw Casey stepping quickly into the room and feeling for the electric button in the wall beside the bedroom door. She sensed rather than heard that door open. She had leaped to her feet and was facing the darkness in that direction. Instinctively, she hurled her flashlight with all her supple young might, and as she writhed out of the window she heard the dull thud with which it struck its mark and the smothered oath it evoked.

And in that same instant that she slipped over the windowsill, her nimble wit told her that Casey would rush to the door and the fire escape, cutting off her retreat, and that she had but one chance of escape.

She crawled quickly along the fire escape in the opposite direction, and finding Casey's bedroom window open, as she expected, slipped quickly through it. Gropingly she found the bed, and crawled beneath it.

Chapter 5

The Whispering Bandit

Under the assumed character of Burrell, Casey had chosen to exhibit no sign of his athletic ability. He played but a mediocre and rather clumsy game of tennis, and at all times held himself under rigid restraint. As a matter of fact, however, he was the possessor of superb strength and agility, and Edna Raalhof, in her boy's clothing, as she crouched beneath his bed, taking stock of her desperate situation, had yet to realize what she had escaped.

Had he been able to reach her, the chances were that she would have been badly battered and crippled before he had discovered or she had been able to apprise him of her sex. For once he launched himself into a physical encounter, his fierce, tearing attack combined all the elements of the skilled boxer, wrestler and rough and tumble fighter, and his instinctive application of them was quicker than thought. It was not without reason that the criminal world with which he came in contact had given him the "monicker" of "Wildcat."

But from the moment she had heard the squeak of the bedsprings, Edna had, it so happened, actually foreseen his movements. That she had not known of his presence in the apartment was due to her failure to investigate his bedroom,

and to his habit of disconnecting his telephone to the mailbox at the main entrance upon retiring, a measure to ensure privacy.

Awaking from a sound sleep, he had gradually become aware of a faint light showing beneath his bedroom door, and had swung himself out of bed to investigate. The sudden disappearance of that glow warned him of the presence of an intruder, and he moved swiftly to the door.

The flashlight, which the girl had hurled, caught him a glancing blow on the side of the head as he reached for the light button, and staggered him for just the instant that she needed to wriggle out of the window.

But in a second, he had recovered himself, flashed on the light and rushed for the door as he drew the obvious conclusion from a glance at the open window.

He failed, however, to find the intruder in the hall, and an inspection of the fire escape did not reveal the expected form scuttling down into the darkness below. He did not care to carry the pursuit further, clad only in his pajamas.

In some puzzlement, he returned to his own quarters. He was almost inclined to attribute the thing to a nightmare, except for the mute evidence of the open window, the flashlight lying on the floor, and the very real sting in his head.

Perhaps, he thought, the burglar had fled up, not down the fire escape. With an exclamation of annoyance that he had failed to look up, he ran into the bedroom and hastily slipped into a pair of trousers and shoes. Taking his automatic, he returned to the other room, and turning off the light to give the impression that he had returned to bed, he pulled a chair over to the window, and after opening the hall door, settled himself to wait for the burglar's return down the fire escape or the stairs, to the annoyance and growing desperation of the girl who lay concealed beneath his bed.

It was not until the first faint touch of grey dawn began to illumine the apartment that he gave up his vigil, and returned to bed, convinced at last that he had been the recipient of a visit from a clever sneak thief who had in some manner outwitted him and made good his escape.

Twenty minutes later, when his regular breathing convinced Edna he had really dropped off to sleep, the girl cautiously drew herself from underneath his bed and softly tiptoed from the room, pausing in the outer room long enough to recover her flashlight and to replace the telltale letter, to which he had paid no attention in the excitement, where she had found it.

Once beyond his door, she threw off her air of caution, and emerged from the apartment house with a carefree air that was as much the result of her relief as assumed. As she round the corner, though, her heart sank again.

A patrolman stood wearily on guard over her machine. If she claimed the apparently abandoned car, some explanation would be in order. She could not ignore him and step into it. And, if she spoke her voice would betray her.

So, showing no interest in the machine or the policeman, she crossed the street diagonally, so as not to pass too close to him, and thrusting her hands in her pockets and pursing her lips in a whistle, she walked briskly on, like any young fellow going forth to an early job. Still nervous from her recent experience, she half-expected a gruff command to give an account of herself, but none was forthcoming, and finally she traversed the length of the block and round the corner.

The situation, she told herself, was not so good. In fact, it was about as desperate as ever. Her disguise had been safe enough in the dark, but she dared not trust herself to it in broad daylight and in close contact with people. Particularly did she shrink from the thought of boarding a trolley car to get back to the country.

And she would have to get back to Clover Hill quickly. Before long the police would take in her abandoned machine, and tracing its ownership by the license number, would be calling up the cottage. She could not afford to have it known that she had been out all night.

An inspiration born of desperation came to her as a dilapidated little automobile came spluttering toward her. A quick glance up and down the street showed it still deserted except for herself and the single occupant of the car, apparently a middle-aged tradesman on his way to the produce market.

Edna ran into the street, gesticulating. The driver pulled up with a puzzled expression. Silently, the supposed youth pointed down the street, and the man's glance followed. He turned again to face the muzzle of an automatic. Trembling, he obeyed the fiercely whispered command to climb down from his seat. Still covering him with the automatic, the youthful appearing bandit, still uttering no word, climbed into the vacated machine, and drove off, leaving him gaping with astonishment and fear.

By the time he recovered his wits enough to make an outcry, and the patrolman who had been standing guard over Edna's machine had come running around the corner, the spluttering little car had disappeared in the opposite direction.

The tradesman cursed complainingly. The policeman figuratively kicked himself. Less than a block and half away Wildcat Casey, the terror of automobile bandits, lay snugly asleep.

The early afternoon papers featured the hold-up by the "the whispering bandit," the proximity of the patrolman at the time, and the fact that the bandit had overlooked a high-priced car which had stood abandoned all night just around the corner.

Luckily for Edna Raalhof, however, the sleepy reporter on early morning assignment, failed to turn in the name of the owner of the abandoned machine, and became the target of some sarcastic remarks on the part of his city editor.

Edna was quite prepared to have the police trace the ownership of the machine. In fact, she was anxious to have them do so and return it, for it was a valuable car. But, she was by no means anxious to have Wildcat Casey putting two and two together concerning it, no matter how little inclined he might be to connect Miss Edna Raalhof, of the Penton Country Club, with the early morning intruder in his apartment.

The exploit of the "Whispering Bandit" also evoked the suspicious interest of Scott Duvenney. The first editions of the evening papers had not reached the street at the hour the lawyer had sauntered into his office. But Cranweiler was there

waiting for him, and Cranweiler had heard of the hold-up a
few hours before by that mysterious young bandit. As in criminal parlance, Duvenney's clients called him their "mouth-
piece," so Duvenney might well have dubbed Cranweiler his
"ears," though the latter ranked in the informal language of
the indefinite fringe of outer legal circles as a "runner." Offi-
cially he was a notary public and an office assistant to the
lawyer. Actually he was the connecting link between
Duvenney and the criminal world from which he drew his
living, and acted as the go-between in most of Duvenney's
dealings with that ring of automobile thieves and bandits
which he had gradually organized and dominated by virtue of
his value to them as an unscrupulous lawyer, and as the
wielder of considerable political power. Cranweiler per-
formed those functions which Duvenney's assumed dignity
would not permit him to do.

Cranweiler was a big man, with an air of bluff geniality
which enabled him to cultivate a wide circle of casual acquaintances both in and out of the police force, and made him valuable to Duvenney as a political as well as a professional aid.

He had been highly flattered by the interest in him which
Edna Raalhof had cleverly allowed him to infer upon the one
occasion, several weeks before, on which she had visited
Duvenney's offices; not that he presumed for a moment to
raise his eyes to such a "queen" as Miss Raalhof, for he had
sense enough to realize that she was "outa his class," and
besides Duvenney "was sweet on her."

Edna had contrived to let him meet her accidentally several times, however, and by delicate hints had conveyed to

him a supposed interest of more than friendly nature in Duvenney, and the idea that she was not so prudish as to be shocked by any revelations he might make to her concerning his employer's affairs. Cranweiler had succumbed utterly to her charm, and had allowed her to "pump" him for far more information than he realized. He felt he was "helping the boss's game," but knew Duvenney's arrogance too well to give him any hint that he was doing it.

"Have you got any line on who this 'whispering bandit' is?" Duvenney asked when Cranweiler told him of the silent hold-up.

"Not a line, boss," Cranweiler replied, shooting the ash from his cigar accurately into a distant spittoon. "It's not one of the boys. I know that."

"How do you know?" snapped the lawyer.

"I been talking to the cop that seen this guy go 'round the corner just before the stick-up. He was a little fellow—couldn't a been more than a hundred and ten or fifteen pounds—and young looking. That description don't tally with any of the boys except Solly Wertheimer, and Solly's in jail, like I told you last night."

At the mention of Wertheimer's name, Duvenney's mind went back to the scene at the Penton Club bar the night before, and Burrell's remark as to the source of the whiskey they had been drinking. Suddenly he leaned aggressively toward Cranweiler.

"There's some funny business going on among the boys, Ed. Some of them are bootlegging on the side. What do you know about it?"

"There isn't any of them would try to get away with that stuff."

"What would you say if I told you Solly Wertheimer and Greasy Gorman actually have been getting away with it, right under our noses? I got a drink last night from a man who got stuff from them."

"Hell!" ejaculated Cranweiler feelingly.

"Have you seen them since they were locked up?"

"Yeah. I was over at City Hall this morning."

"Have they got any money?"

"Not a nickel."

"Tell them to get another lawyer. I'm done with them."

"Say boss, that's a little rough, ain't it?" asked Cranweiler doubtfully.

"It's no rougher than their bootlegging on the side and holding out on me. I'm not going to let any of the boys double-cross me that way. A stretch up the river will teach 'em where they get off with that stuff. No, you go tell them I'm done, Ed. Then scratch them off the list." Then, as Cranweiler reached for his hat, Duvenney added, "And keep your eye peeled for this 'whispering bandit.' If he's pinched, you've got to see him first and line him up for me. It may be worthwhile to invest a reasonable amount of bail in him. One more thing. Get a hold of Pearson and Whitey Beaman. I want my percentage of that job they pulled out on Old Hickory Road last night."

Duvenney turned to opening his mail in a decidedly irritable mood. It was bad enough that Wertheimer and Gorman had blundered into the clutches of Casey and had been arrested with no funds available for their defense. It was worse that they had, as he believed, engaged in any enterprise without sharing profits with him. He began to wonder how much more of this sort of thing was going on. The seeds of suspicion which Casey, in the character of Burrell, had sown in his mind the night before, were beginning to sprout.

His annoyance was only increased when Cranweiler returned, later in the morning, with the news that Pearson and Whitey Beaman would have no percentage to split with him, because they had both been arrested by State troopers before they had been able to get back to the city with their loot.

This was bad, Duvenney thought. He was likely to lose two more good men. It would mean that they would be arraigned outside the city, where his influence was only indirect, and would have to stand trail in the Compton county court. Cursing them for their clumsiness in being caught with the stolen goods still in their possession, and remembering with uneasiness the incident of the car which had followed him to the scene of the hold-up, Duvenney grabbed his hat and started for the office of the District Attorney, through whom he hoped to have the men remanded to the city authorities. Perhaps he could persuade the District Attorney to "want" them on some trumped up prior charge. Then he might have a low bail fixed and let them jump it, or have the charges dismissed with the possibility that they might elude the county detectives on their release.

In the street below he almost collided with a figure which he did not know had been waiting patiently for his appearance.

"Hello there, Burrell," he said. "Sorry I can't stop now, old man. Got an engagement with the District Attorney."

He would have been puzzled had he known that the supposed Burrell entered the building immediately and ascended to the fifth floor offices of Scott Duvenney, to ask if Mr. Duvenney were in.

Chapter 6

Through the Window

"Is Mr. Duvenney in?" inquired Casey of the young woman who sat at the typewriter desk in the outer office. At the same time, taking the liberty that might be expected of an old acquaintance, he stepped quickly across the room to the open door of the inner office and glanced in. Ed Cranweiler stood looking out the window there, and did not notice him.

But neither was Casey looking at Cranweiler. His glance roved quickly over the entire office, resting momentarily upon the telephone box screwed on the wall beside Duvenney's desk. That wall, he noticed, was the one which separated Duvenney's suite from the next office down the corridor.

"Mr. Duvenney isn't in," the girl was saying. To herself she whispered; "Some nerve!"

"What time will he be back?" asked Casey.

"He didn't leave word," she replied.

"He won't be back for an hour at least," Cranweiler volunteered, coming into the outer office, "He's gone to the District Attorney's office. Gimme your name and I'll tell him you called."

"Oh, it's not important," Casey explained. "I just

stopped in to have a personal chat with him. I'll call him up later."

He chuckled to himself as he stepped again into the corridor.

Almost immediately after there breezed into the office a man with a somewhat grimy face and clad in working clothes.

"Telephone company," he vouchsafed laconically, throwing back his coat to give the girl a glimpse of a badge, and swinging from his shoulder a strap on which were suspended a telephone box and a couple of 'phones.' "Central reports trouble on this line."

There was something in his smile and stare which caused the girl quickly to avoid his glance, though puzzled by the vague familiarity of his face, and assume an air of dignity.

"The telephone is in the other room," she said curtly.

Briskly he went to work. Taking up the instrument on Duvenney's desk, while the girl kept a wary eye on him, he apparently went through the usual careless preliminary test conversation with "central." But he held it in such a way that the stenographer could not notice he was holding down the receiver hook with his finger. He asked central to give him a ring on the line. He grunted when none was forthcoming and went to work at once on the box. Deftly he disconnected the wire and removed it, substituting the new one he carried. He found it necessary to bore new holes in the wall to attach it. But the girl in the outer office could not see that he was boring these holes clear through the wall, and that it was short ends of disconnected wires that he put through these holes instead of screws. The new box quickly attached, he slung his paraphernalia over his shoulder, and in her confusion under the stare with which he favored her as he passed out, she failed to notice that he had not made the customary closing test to report the line in order.

According to the records of the telephone company, the adjoining office was occupied by one Samuel T. Jones. So also, it was on the records of the agent for the building, and according to the lettering on the door. It had recently been leased. The telephone company had a record of it because it had installed a private wire, at a handsome price, between the office and the apartment of the said Samuel T. Jones. What the company's records did not show is that the supposed apartment of Samuel T. Jones was actually leased in the name of Theodore Burrell, and that the supposed Theodore Burrell was none other than Patrick J. Casey. The company had no way of finding these things out, and no motive for trying to.

And since the private wire did not pass through a switch-board, and the supposed Mr. Jones having paid handsomely for it, the company did not know nor care if it was left open all the time.

So when he entered the office next to Duvenney's, Casey had only to connect up the loose ends of the Dictaphone wires, from the telephone box he had just installed in Duvenney's office, to the private wire, wash up, change his clothes and go back to his room to sit in comfort and listen to any conversation that went on in Duvenney's office, at any time he chose.

He grinned as he sat that afternoon and made copious notes of Duvenney's affairs for possible future reference. But it so happened that nothing transpired in connection with the case of the banditry and thefts on which Casey was working until late in the afternoon, when Duvenney took up his telephone and called a Clover Hill number.

"Let me speak to Miss Raalhof, please," Casey heard the lawyer say. "Oh, is that you Edna—No indeed, I have no intention of calling it off. The chance to be alone with you comes so seldom that it is very precious—Now that is not fair. You know I did not mean that. I—It would be too precious under any circumstances to think of sacrificing—I called up to find out just when you expect me—At seven-thirty?—I certainly shall—Good-bye."

Casey whistled his surprise. There had been a subtle change from the lawyer's customary tones in that conversation that told the detective much. Finesse was not Duvenney's forte. The man was clever. He was wary, keen and quick of comprehension. But he was aggressive and domineering, by no means subtle in his methods. There had been a pleading humility in his voice, just a touch of it, that was totally unexpected. The only thing that could account for it was that the man was sincerely in love.

It was a revelation of a human side to an otherwise hard character and Casey's reaction to it would have surprised himself had he paused to consider it. It should have raised the man a bit in his estimation. It should have put him on a plane of a more respected antagonist. But it didn't. Casey found himself hating the man more cordially than before. And it was with a curse of annoyance that he finally turned away from the telephone upon the realization that Duvenney had left his office and began to dress for dinner.

He turned his attention to a matter which had been in the back of his head all day, the burglarious visit to his apartment during the early morning hours.

Upon arising that morning he had made a thorough examination of the place, which had told him much. To begin with, he had found his bedroom window open wide, whereas it had only been half open when he had retired. There was evidence in the desk that his papers had been gone through pretty thoroughly. And the letter signed, "Charley" had been among them. He paused in the middle of his struggle with his dress tie, and went to the desk to look at the letter again. No, there was nothing in it to look suspicious upon a casual examination. It was not part of Casey's plan to let his real identity be found out. Yet had the letter been subjected only to casual scrutiny? Apparently the burglar had given his whole attention to the desk, not to search for valuables. Did this not argue that he had been hunting for information? What kind of information? Carefully Casey went over his recent life as Theodore Burrell and the only thing he could think of that could possibly have invited such a visit was a suspicion as to his identity.

Alarmed now by the threat to the success of his campaign against Duvenney and his criminal organization, he made another and more careful examination of the apartment. He could not afford to have his visitor inform Duvenney that Burrell was in reality Wildcat Casey. He must find the fellow somehow and manage to silence him. To the best of his recollection, from the shadowy glimpse he had gotten of the figure outlined for an instant against the window, he was a little fellow, of slight build and he had slipped over the windowsill with surprising agility.

This time he paid more attention to his bedroom, for the thought flashed upon him that in it might lie the explanation of the burglar's sudden disappearance. He could have slipped through the window into the bedroom instead of running up or down the fire escape.

Carefully he examined the windowsill. There seemed to be a spot where the slight accumulation of dust had been wiped away, as though somebody had passed in or out. Then he went over the glass in the window inch by inch, catching the reflections from all angles. With an exclamation of satisfaction, he noted five faint but clear impressions of fingertips on the outside of the glass. These he examined with a magnifying glass, making notation of the loops and whirls. They were the imprints of very small, delicate fingers; more like a woman's than a man's he thought.

He would wire C. M. Haige, chief of the criminal investigation and prosecution department of the insurance association, and the "Charley" of the communication in his desk, asking him to find out if they belonged to any crook with a police record, and if so to have that crook taken up at once, even if it had to be on a trumped up charge. If he could be held for a few weeks out of communication with Duvenney all would be well. Casey did not want to make his request directly to the police, as he had already uncovered evidences of a leak somewhere in the department, and if Duvenney learned that the fellow had been arrested at the behest either of Theodore Burrell or Casey, the whole purpose of the arrest would be frustrated.

At the Ritz he sent his wire, then strolled into the grill with copies of several of the evening papers under his arm. As he ate he skimmed through them, quickly singling out all articles which touched upon the subject of automobile thefts or hold ups.

There was a small "follow up" on the case of the "whispering bandit." The tradesman's car had been found, it seemed, abandoned on the Old Hickory Road three miles west of Burville. That would be somewhere in the vicinity of Clover Hill, Casey noted mentally. There were several other items in the same paper, of casual but not immediate interest to him.

It was in another sheet that he found a little story, tucked away beneath a murder trial. It told of the recovery by the police of a car which had been stolen from the garage of Sigmund Raalhof, of Clover Hill.

Casey's eyes widened a bit. It was as though a number of unrelated thoughts had clicked together in a perfect combination, without volition on his part. These sudden flashes of intuition came to him at times, and he had learned by experience to set high value on them.

Slowly and gently he folded his paper and laid it beside his plate, staring at his baked potato in a manner which caused uneasiness to his observant waiter.

The Raalhof car had been found practically on the spot where the whispering bandit had stolen the other one. The trademan's car had been found within a comparatively short distance of the place where the Raalhof car was alleged to have been stolen. The Raalhof car had been found, and the trademan's car had been stolen, within a short distance of Casey's own apartment. The description of the "whispering bandit" tallied in so far as he was said to be a short youth of slight build, with his own vague glimpse of the burglar who had rummaged through his desk, not for valuables, but for information.

The bandit was a mystery to Casey. It could not have been Sigmund Raalhof, for he was a big man. Nor did the Raalhof's have a chauffeur.

But aside from the identity of the bandit, the suspicion shrieked aloud in Casey's mind of a menacing connection between himself and some person in, or in the vicinity of the Raalhofs. And Duvenney, the quarry he was stalking, was to see Edna Raalhof that night!

Could that girl, with her indefinable charm and some-times world-weary eyes, be connected with this thing in any way? Casey hated to think it. But at any rate there was only one thing for him to do, and that was to transport himself to the scene of activity as quickly as possible. When he got there he would see what he should see.

Tossing a bill, much too large, to the astonished waiter, he hurried from the grill, and took a taxi to the garage where he kept his own car.

In a remarkably short space of time he had run his car, with lights out, up the driveway of a vacant property two doors from the Raalhofs, where in the shadow of the trees it could not be seen, and inwardly cursing the necessity of keeping on his overcoat to hide the expanse of his dress shirt, he dodged quickly through the back hedges toward the Raalhof cottage, where a thin edge of light showed beneath the drawn shade of one of the dining room windows. Drawing himself up until his eyes were on a level with it, he gazed in.

Accustomed as he was to startling denouncements, what he saw made him gasp.

Chapter 7

Masks Aside

If there was anything lacking in the spell which Edna Raalhof had cast over Scott Duvenney, she remedied it that night.

Weary from a day of adversity and worry such as he had not known for many long months, his self-sufficiency, aggressiveness and hardness was at very low pressure. The fact that Duvenney's activities were decidedly open to criticism on both moral and ethical grounds in no way made him less susceptible to strain than other men, and so it was with a feeling of relaxation not unmixed with a craving for sympathy that he awaited the appearance of his hostess.

The soft glow of shaded lamps and the flutter of a recently lit fire, together with the various little touches of a feminine hand which the Raalhof library evidenced, was in comfortable contrast with the chill of the deepening twilight without.

Following the custom of the Penton Club set, Duvenney had come in formal evening dress. He was prepared for a vision of some brilliant décolletage. Instead, Edna entered clad in a neat little skirt and a waist, the severity of which was relieved only by the silken softness of its material. He had been expecting the splendor of sophistication, but he found in her the simplicity of youth. For an instant he had what was almost a twinge of conscience that he wanted this girl to link her life to his.

"You are a model guest, Scott," she laughed, glancing at the clock and extending her hand, which she allowed him to retain for the fraction of a second. "You are on time to the minute."

"I am afraid I can't give the credit to manners, but rather to the attraction," he said.

"How very sweet of you to say that. But come, Mazie has our supper waiting." And oddly enough, for the man that he was, Duvenney thrilled a bit at her use of the words "sweet" and "our."

At the table, however, she cleverly anticipated his several attempts to discuss what was uppermost in his mind, until he finally surrendered the intention for the moment that gave himself over to the pleasurable consciousness of her presence, following but vaguely the inconsequential channels into which she guided the conversation.

Not until they were seated before the fire in the library, and Mazie's "Good night, Miss Edna" had been followed by the distant click of the back door latch, did she raise the barrage of trivialities with which she had held at a distance.

In the silence which ensued, Duvenney lifted his gaze from the fire. From the depths of an easy chair Edna was regarding him fixedly. Her expression, being of the sort sometimes called "inscrutable" or "unfathomable," thrilled him again.

But his own look gave him away, and before he could marshall his words to launch the plea which he had promised himself was going to sweep the girl's resistance before it, she spoke.

"Scott," she said in a level, serious tone, "I want you to tell me all about your practice."

At any other time he would have regarded such a demand as an impertinence, and no one knew it better than Edna herself, who had calculated carefully every little detail of the evening with the view to certain definite effects.

"My practice?" he countered in surprise. "What—"

"Yes," she said. "Are not most of your clients crooks—particularly automobile thieves and bandits, thugs, gunmen and bootleggers?"

Duvenney was puzzled. What was the girl driving at?

"Why—er—yes, I suppose they are. But surely a girl with your knowledge of the world should not hold that against me, Edna. When a man takes up the practice of criminal law he cannot very well avoid taking the cases of criminals, can he? You know the law does not deny even to habitual criminals the right to employ counsel for their own defense. No man can be prejudged guilty, before—"

"Yes, yes, Scott, I know all that. But these criminal clients of yours; they pay you very big fees, don't they?"

For an instant he thought he saw her purpose. She was not finding fault with the character of his practice. She was, he felt, trying to inform herself as to his "prospects." It gave him a twinge now, as it had not the night before, to think that she was interested so cannily in his financial status. Still he wanted her, whether she came to him for his money or himself.

"Neither the size nor the frequency of the fees, Edna, leave anything to be desired," he went on with relief. "I think I can say, with all due modesty, that I have been very successful. Yes, very successful."

"They pay you percentages out of the loot they take, don't they?"

Duvenney gasped in spite of himself. The girl, her chin resting in her cupped hand, was gazing straight into his eyes with a baffling, impersonal expression.

"Well—you see," he floundered, "I don't know where—that is to say, it is none of my business where their money—"

He stopped short at her smile. This time she was not acting, and it was a twisted little smile, half cynical, half humorous. This time, too, he fathomed her eyes, reading in their depths a weary knowledge of evil.

"Let's drop our poses for tonight, Scott," she said. "I assure you, my friend, I am no 'simp moll,' nor likely to become one."

He gasped again, at her use of crooks' slang, which fell so oddly from the little lips whose enunciation was perfect.

"You have taken me for an adventuress," she went on, "but really, Scott, you don't know me at all. Of course you gained certain impressions of me the night I let you 'pick me up'—I believe that is the vulgar expression—at the Ritz. First you thought I was, well, not a very nice girl. Then you found I wasn't what you thought, and you were puzzled. Finally you came to the conclusion that I was just a nobody of a girl, with sufficient cleverness and knowledge of the world to put on a stupendous front while I angled for a rich husband. When you introduced father and me at the Penton Club you had some sort of vague idea that you might use me in some manner to further your interests. Then your interest became gradually more personal, and as it grew greater your judgment grew less. Now you would like to possess me. You would give almost any price to."

Duvenney, dazed by her directness, could but gulp an eager assent.

"You've got me wrong, Scott," she went on relentlessly, "and, paradoxically, you're not going to get me at all. No, do not interrupt me yet. We'll leave that part of it for the moment.

"Now as to yourself. You are a criminal lawyer in both senses of the word. You are a crook, Scott Duvenney. You have under your thumb a highly efficient organization of crooks. You are its fountain head. You make its plans, guide its activities, and rake in the lion's share of the loot. It is you who prepare the alibis, pull the political wires and guide the distribution of the graft which makes the police blind and careless when it comes to gathering evidence. It is you who wield a power little short of life and death over your followers. If one of them becomes rebellious you have only to withdraw your patronage from him, and he is swept from existence by the zeal of the authorities and his own inability to play a lone hand successfully against the organized forces of society. Is this not all true?"

Duvenney leaped to his feet.

"Edna," he exclaimed, "I don't understand what you are driving at. Girl, do you realize that what I am offering you is honorable marriage?"

"Scott," she replied, "I am trying to tell you that what you offer is impossible. No man will ever claim me. I don't want your protection. I don't want your attentions." A glitter that held him spellbound came into her eyes. "Scott Duvenney," she said, "what I expect from you is acknowledgement of supremacy and obedience!"

Suddenly, the man regained his self control. He dropped into his chair, threw back his head and laughed boisterously. As suddenly he stopped.

"Why?" he shot the question at her.

"Because," she replied, with an air of weary patience, "I will ruin you if you do not."

"How?" he snapped.

"There are many possibilities," she said, and smiled slowly. "There is, for instance, the police."

"I own them."

"Or perhaps the District Attorney."

"I own him too."

"The newspapers."

"They have done all they could to me already. They have no evidence."

"I might supply them with some," Edna hinted. She was still smiling, but now there was real amusement in her eyes, and he found it maddening.

"I should call it blackmail—a frame-up by a clever adventuress. Your past is a mystery, Edna. You couldn't put it over."

Edna rose and stood a moment gazing pensively at the fire which outlined her graceful silhouette. Even in his anger at her and his vague apprehension, born of her perfect confidence, he could not help admiring her poise. What a girl she was! Not a thing in her manner indicated that she had boldly locked wills with him in an attempt to batter away his defenses and reduce him to the same state of subjection in which he held the band of crooks upon whom he preyed.

"Yes, you are right about that," she admitted frankly, and added with a whimsical little glance, "There are mysteries in my past which Scotland Yard would give much to know, mysteries which the customs officials on this side of the ocean have never solved, mysteries in Paris which still remain mysteries to the police, and mysteries in Berlin which the military police never even had a chance to fathom. Do you remember, last year, how a certain priceless necklace vanished from among the crown jewels of Italy?

"That was a mistake, however. Such things are too difficult to dispose of, and too dangerous to keep. No, my friend. Banish that sly look from your eyes. I haven't got the necklace—now.

"But to return to the matter in hand. Suppose I suggest an alternative, Scott. Suppose, instead of giving my information to the police or the District Attorney, or the newspapers, I give it to—ah—a certain gentleman known as Wildcat Casey?"

Duvenney went white. Casey had become a real terror to him. Already he had captured four of Duvenney's "clients," and under such peculiar circumstances that Duvenney was powerless to help them. That afternoon the state police had balked the effort of the District Attorney to obtain custody of the bandits who had held up the Malason machine. Duvenney feared that no matter how cleverly he might defend himself, Casey might nevertheless reduce him to a state of impotency by landing his whole organization behind the bars. The man was always so unexpectedly adroit in staging his captures in spectacular fashion, with all the necessary evidence gathered neatly together, and usually with witnesses of such a character that it was impossible to suppress any of it.

"Then again," Edna went on, "I might decide to handle you all by myself, Scott." And imperious mockery crept into her gaze.

Desperate, and suddenly conscious of the humiliation she was heaping upon him, Duvenney leaped to his feet. Who was this girl to scorn and threaten him, to try to dominate him. His passion swept away his last shreds of self control.

For a moment he stood glaring, but she did not quail, meeting his look with that same mockery. Then the elemental brute in him rose to the surface.

With an inarticulate snarl of rage, he lunged toward her.

Chapter 8

Defiance

The scene which met Wildcat Casey's eyes as he drew up to the level of the window sill was enough to astonish him.

It was at this instant that in a paroxysm of rage the lawyer leaped at Edna Raalhof. Casey's first instinct was to drop back to the ground and seek an entrance to the house as quickly as possible. But a glance at the girl prevented him.

Edna did not shrink. In fact, she stepped lithely forward to meet the lawyer's attack. What followed happened in less than a second.

She seized one of the talon-like hands, outstretched to grasp her, with both of her own. With a sinuous motion of lightning-like rapidity she twisted around, crouched, and with a vicious tug, added to the momentum of the man's rush, threw him completely over her head.

The jar with which the man crashed to the floor, rattled the window through which Casey was looking. Her breast heaving a bit from the exertion, Edna stood looking at him, the mocking smile still on her lips. Duvenney stirred slowly and groaned.

Casey waited for no more. Letting go of the window sill, he ran around the house, seeking an open window or an unlocked door. On the other side of the house, he found a dining room window half open, and promptly launched himself through it. He found a hiding place behind the heavy draperies which separated that room from the library.

Duvenney, still half-stunned from his fall, was painfully climbing to his feet.

"You she-devil!" he growled malevolently between clenched teeth. "I'll get you for this. Don't you think I won't."

Edna said nothing, but her eyes glittered. She took a swift step toward him. He shrank back hurriedly.

"You'll get what I choose to give you," she laughed scornfully, "and no more. Perhaps you'll admit now that I can handle you, without recourse to Casey or anybody else. Now what's your answer, yes or no? Quick! I have no more time to waste with you, Scott Duvenney."

"It's 'yes,'" he growled reluctantly. He betrayed an uncomfortable desire to be going.

"Good," the girl snapped. "But let me warn you, you have just now made a bargain which you cannot break. If you try it, I'll break you—physically, and with my two hands if need be."

Behind the curtains, Casey wondered for an instant if his senses had left him. The girl was so slender. She seemed hardly more than a child beside Duvenney. Yet here she was, cowing him into groveling submission by sheer physical ability and the fierceness of her will. The situation was unbelievable.

Edna was still talking, her words evidently stinging the man like the lash of a whip.

"I can follow you wherever you go, Scott Duvenney.

Don't try the stratagem of a hunting trip to escape. Oh, I know your mind is already at work devising some plan to avoid submission. You can't run away. You can't ask the police for protection against a mere slip of a girl. You can't 'frame' me either. Could you persuade a jury against me? I think not. And don't try to send your thugs against me with any 'strong-arm' tactics. I assure you I can handle them as easily as I did you."

"How did you—" began Duvenney.

"How did I find out so much about you? From your thugs, my dear man. I know every move that you and they have made in the past two weeks. In the organization of your forces you have guarded carefully against all but one thing. Money could not have made one of them squeal on you, Scott, for you hold the threat of prison over them. Fear of the law could not have accomplished it either, for they fear you still more. But feminine charm is a very subtle weapon. Not one of them knows that he has 'double-crossed' you yet.

"Then why don't I fling you aside completely and assume leadership openly? Simply because I need your legal and political strength, and I know I can keep you whopped in line." Slowly she stepped toward him until he was brought up against the wall, and could back away no farther. "And don't forget, Scott Duvenney, that at the first false step you make I can, if I so choose, snuff out your very life, like that!" And she snapped her fingers under his nose. "The sword will be constantly above your head, and I shall have my own method of cutting the thread that suspends it. Even should you be so foolhardy as to think you could have me shot down in the dark without warning, it will cut you down. Now go!" She pointed dramatically toward the door.

Hurriedly Duvenney slunk through it, unwittingly brushing against the concealed detective.

At the sound of the front door closing, Edna's tense attitude relaxed, and she sank into a chair. After a bit, elusive dimples appeared at the corners of her mouth. Then she smiled, and finally laughed outright.

Casey took advantage of her preoccupation to slip away from the curtains. Silently he crossed the dining room and climbed out the window again.

He might have followed Duvenney. In one sense it would have been the logical thing to do. He decided against it, however. Edna Raalhof now stood revealed to him in an entirely new character.

"I've got Duvenney's number," he reflected. "But, there's a devil of a lot about this girl that I don't understand yet, and quite clearly the little lady is to be reckoned with. I can smash Duvenney whenever I'm ready, but I have nothing on her—yet."

He glanced at the phosphorescent dial of his watch. It was not too late, he decided, for a call.

He dodged back across the lawns to his car. Then, driving it out into the road he came to a stop at the Raalhof gate, and mentally assuming his character of Ted Burrell, crunched up the gravel walk and rang the bell. Edna, herself, came to the door.

There was sudden apprehension in the first swift glance

she gave him, then genuine pleasure as she flung the door wide.

"Awfully brazen of me to drop in this way without warning, Miss Raalhof," he said, pausing in the doorway, "but the fact is I was driving over to South Hills, and I couldn't resist the temptation to extend my sympathies for your experience of last night, and assure myself that it hadn't upset you too much."

"Well, now that you've gotten this far, won't you take off your coat and come in for a few minutes?" she said, and without waiting for his reply led the way to the library.

Casey accepted the suggestion with but perfunctory protest, smiling inwardly as he slipped out of his light overcoat and followed. This was going to be an interesting little contest of wills, he felt. Unless all his instinct had failed him, this girl had seen through his alias, and knew him for Wildcat Casey. Considering his advent so soon after the departure of Duvenney, she ought to be considerably on edge. It remained to be seen what he could draw out of her while she tried to figure out what he knew.

She stood by the fire smiling as he came into the room. He noted, however, that her expression was quite different from that with which she had favored Duvenney. Even then, he could scarcely grasp the contrast. The chair which Duvenney had upset in his fall had been righted, he noticed, and all but a few particles of the shattered vase which had been jarred from its pedestal had been picked up and cast into the fireplace.

Quick as his glance had been, however, she was as quick

to notice it. It was natural for him to look at the fire. But, he would not have looked instantly at that chair unless he knew what had just happened.

"Do you ever succumb to eavesdropping, Mr. Burrell?" she asked quickly.

From the genuine amusement in her smile she might have been teasing him about some trivial matter. Casey couldn't help grinning.

"Quite often," he admitted frankly. "One hears—and sees—such interesting things."

"But one is so often disillusioned also," she remarked, her head turned aside. It was typical of her that she offered no defense or explanation of what she knew he had seen.

"Yes, that also," he remarked simply.

For a while, neither spoke. Edna sat gazing at the fire, her profile toward Casey; and he was looking at her. Then, she looked up.

"I don't feel a bit upset about being held up last night," she said. "Through your efforts, Mr. Casey, the bandits were captured and I recovered my rings. I owe you my thanks for that."

"So," he said, "it's to be masks off. So be it. Exit Burrell. Enter Casey."

"Alias Wildcat," supplied Edna. "Honestly, I'm sorry. Mr. Burrell was such an agreeable companion at the club, you know, while Mr. Casey is—"

"Impossible, of course. But then, you see, the Miss Raalhof whom Burrell knew is not all the same Miss Raalhof with whom Casey is acquainted."

"Partially acquainted," corrected Edna. Again she was gazing into the fire. Casey lapsed into silence. Once she glanced up at him, only to avert her eyes immediately. Finally, she straightened up in her chair and turned toward him with a toss of her head.

"But I don't see why I should explain anything to you," she said, as though continuing a previously unspoken train of thought. "You're just a private detective. You're not even connected to the police. And I'm—well, I'm what I am, and what I'm going to continue to be.

"So far as the police know, I am Edna Raalhof, and that's all. So far as you know, I'm Edna Raalhof, and—athletic."

"May I add, burglarious and banditic?"

"Oh," she said, flashing him a look of surprised admiration. "You figured that out too, did you?"

Again Casey grinned.

"Well," she asked irritably, after waiting for him to speak, "why don't you say something? Why don't you threaten to arrest me unless I get out of town? Why don't you tell me I'm too sweet and intelligent a girl to live a life of crime? Why don't you try to reform me?"

"Would the effort be of any avail?" he asked, still smiling.

Edna leaped to her feet, her hands clenched.

"That's what you were thinking about anyhow," she blazed. "You're just like the rest of the hypocrites. You call me a crook. But these pampered, brainless simps, immersed in the mockery of their conventional little lives, who'd roll their eyes in shocked prudery at the thought of stealing a nickel, but who steal the reputations of their neighbors, and tear each other's morals to pieces like a pack of hungry hyenas—you call them nice girls." She put a world of scorn into the outburst.

"I think I had better be going," Casey said softly. He arose and stood looking down at her. She seemed such a child, flushed with the vehemence of her unexpected tirade. "I'm not going to try to threaten or persuade you into anything. I know quite well that it would be useless. But," he added simply, "if I catch you with the goods I shall run you in."

Moved by a strange impulse, he extended his hand. For a bare instant she hesitated, then took it. In the pressure of their grip there was something of mutual understanding and respect.

As he released her hand, however, the incongruity of it all assailed him, and in spite of himself he could not wholly conceal the smile which struggled to his lips and eyes, even though an inner sense warned him it was like lighting a cigarette in a powder magazine.

He moved to the door, and there, ill at ease, he turned to say good-bye.

He looked into the muzzle of an automatic, which she held unwaveringly.

Chapter 9

The "Wildcat" Leaps

"Put 'em up!" Edna commanded in terse, icy tones.

At the fierce gleam which supplanted the first surprise in his eyes she tensed her finger on the trigger.

"Perhaps you did not hear me," she snapped. "I requested you to hold up your hands."

"No," he said quietly, but made no move. His expression now was one which her father would have admired across a poker table.

"You sneak! You saw what happened to that man Duvenney, didn't you?" She approached him as she spoke, cautiously, like some sleek young tigress.

"But I'm not Duvenney," he explained.

"I'm not afraid of you, Casey," she said. "See!" and stepping quickly forward she stuck the automatic within a few inches of his nose, her little jaw thrust forward in determination. "Put–up–your–hands!" She ground the words out between her teeth.

This time he said nothing, but gazed steadily and inscrutably into her eyes, ignoring the fascination of the automatic's muzzle.

For ages, it seemed to him, they stood there, their wills

locked in contest.

At last, though his eyes could detect no change in her expression nor wavering in the hand that held the weapon, his nerves, raw with the strain, sensed his victory.

"I know you are not afraid of me," he answered her then, "but you can't shoot."

Gently he raised his hand and took the gun from her unresisting fingers.

"It might go off by accident," he explained.

As though hypnotized she watched him as he stepped to the table and laid it there.

At this juncture a slight sound at the hall doorway caused them both to turn quickly.

Sigmund Raalhof stood there, and in his hand was a revolver. He had entered the house unheard by either of them, and after gazing a moment in astonishment, had acted.

"I have you covered, Burrell," he said. "Now don't move an inch toward that gun on the table, but put up your hands. I can, and will shoot, if you don't. Now I think, sir, that an explanation of why I find you here threatening my daughter is in order." But he glanced at Edna, not at Casey, for the explanation.

Fleeting as that shift of his eyes was, Casey took advantage of it. With the agility of a wild cat he leaped aside and in the same instant ducked. Twice Raalhof's revolver spat fire, and missed its target, which was moving faster than his trigger finger could coordinate with his brain.

Then the detective was upon him, a flying avalanche of elbows, knees and fists. Staggering back under the fury of his rush, Raalhof slipped and fell. But he hit the floor—a crashing blow on the point of the chin—which robbed him of consciousness. Casey with a lurch to one side had thrown himself clear of the stream of bullets which Edna, who had snatched up her automatic from the table, hurled after him.

His mind, racing now, grasped the danger of his situation. That fusillade could not go unnoticed in the neighborhood. In a few moments men would be running toward the house from all directions. If captured, what could be easier than for Edna and her father to charge him with attempted burglary and assault. His word as Theodore Burrell, a personality unknown to the Raalhofs' neighbors, would hardly avail against the joint accusation of father and daughter, and the very patent evidence in the battering he had given the man.

Even granted time, he would have to do more than prove his identity as Wildcat Casey to clear himself. He would have to prove them crooks, for private detectives, as a class, bore no saintly reputations. He had nothing better than a clever guess to incriminate either of them, and it would be fatal to his plans to be lodged in jail, even for a few days, while Edna Raalhof and Duvenney were free to pursue their activities.

This thought flashed upon him even as he dashed through the dining room toward the window by which he had first made his entrance to the house. Edna followed.

At the window his figure appeared for an instant in silhouette. The girl squeezed the trigger of her automatic, but with no more result than a click. She had exhausted the magazine. Then he was gone.

Minus hat and overcoat, a wild figure in his mussed dress

suit and torn collar, he leaped into his machine and set his foot on the starter. The engine coughed, spat, then took hold. With a jerk he let in the clutch, driving straight for a man who leaped into the center of the road, then quickly dodged. The hubbub of shouting, in which was mixed the shrill note of a police whistle, died away behind him.

Speeding through the night, with no sound but the purring hum of his powerful motor, he mentally balanced his ledgers for the day. Chargeable to loss was the exposure of his identity to Edna Raalhof, and the necessity of abandoning his rooms, with the recently connected wire leading to the Dictaphone in Duvenney's office. If the girl should tell Duvenney—and he dared not risk the chance that she wouldn't—the lawyer would seize the opportunity to bring about his arrest on charges preferred by the Raalhofs. He would have to "disappear," and revise his plans for completing his chain of evidence.

As a gain he could list the fact that he has ascertained definitely that the girl had visited his rooms and discovered his identity. It was something to know this, instead of to merely suspect that some unknown person had done it. Also, there was the amazing disclosure of Edna Raalhof's true character, and the fact that in some manner she was active in the case.

On the whole, he felt that the advantages overbalanced the losses. There was no telling how the girl, working in the dark, might have upset his plans when he least expected it.

But what was her game? He swore softly to himself at his failure to arrive in time to overhear the whole of her talk with Duvenney.

The chill rush of the night air brought Casey back to consider action of his present situation. Bringing his car to a stop, he drew from a compartment beneath the seat a raincoat and cap. As he put them on a plan began to take form in his mind, one in which time played an important part.

Duvenney, he knew lived in a quiet residence section just inside the city line, where he maintained a fairly extensive establishment in charge of a competent housekeeper. The house stood by itself with some little ground around it. Such being the case, Casey figured, it ought not be difficult to find where the telephone wires entered the building and to cut them, for as a rule in wiring such houses the line is brought down one of the walls and led into the basement.

He seated himself once more behind the wheel, and throwing caution to the winds, opened the throttle wide, slowing down only when within a short distance of his destination.

At the nearest corner he passed a patrolman, who turned perfunctorily to watch his machine. With a muttered imprecation at this piece of ill luck, the investigator determined that a bold course would be safest. He drew up openly therefore in front of Duvenney's house, and walked hurriedly up the walk, as though on a hasty errand.

Reaching a section deep in the shadow of several trees, he dodged rapidly aside, and began running lightly around the house. In the rear he found the wires. It took but a moment to saw through them with his pocketknife, and dodge back to the front of the house, and in the shelter of the shadows to reach the entrance, just as the heavy step of the patrolman turned in at the gate.

Assuming an aid of reluctant disappointment, Casey turned to meet him, glancing back a couple of times at the darkened windows.

"Can you tell me," he asked "if this is where Mr. Duvenney, the lawyer, lives?" He took a piece of paper from his pocket and pretended to look at it.

"It is," said the policeman, scrutinizing him carefully, then apparently satisfied with Casey's appearance, "But you'll not find him home for some time yet, I'm thinking. Mr. Duvenney does not keep early hours. He's off somewhere tonight in his dress suit."

"Oh well," said Casey. "I can phone him," he sauntered back to his machine as the patrolmen stepped up to the front door to try it. Casey had little fear that even if the man did go around to the back of the house he would spot the slight gap in the wires.

Now, Casey told himself, he would be safe for a few hours. He could return to his apartment, secure a bit of rest, prepare for his disappearance as Theodore Burrell, and listen in on his Dictaphone line for any attempt Edna might possibly make to communicate with him, safe in the knowledge that she could not reach him anywhere but at his office over the telephone.

It was about nine-thirty in the morning that the conversation he was expecting took place.

"Hello," he heard Duvenney snap; and then in a sulkier tone, "Oh, is that you Edna?—What do you mean? —Well—er—now, you don't really expect that a man like myself would willingly surrender his independence so completely as all that, do you?—Huh? (This in a startled tone)—Why—er —damnation! I haven't got any choice, have I? I'll have to agree—All right, it's a deal then. Who is he?—Ted Burrell?—Gad! I always thought there was something about that fellow that was funny—Well, what do you want me to do?—(long pause)— Burglary and assault with intent to kill, we'll call it. I'll have him pinched inside of half an hour. Once behind the bars it'll take him several days to prove his identity, and even then it's a safe bet I can have him jugged for keeps. Huh! Pretty coarse work, that. I don't see where that bird got his reputation. Any saphead of a police detective would have better sense than to try that kind of rough stuff. Well, that'll give us plenty of time, anyhow. And you'll drop in here at the office to talk things over?—All right then, good bye."

In his apartment the supposed Theodore Burrell grinned, and started to hang up the receiver. But the sound which came from it before he broke the connection caused him to listen intently again.

Duvenney was conversing in low tones, apparently with his satellite Cranweiler, concerning the division of spoils obtained by two members of the gang in a hold up the night before.

"I can't get out there until tonight, I tell you," the lawyer was saying. "I didn't bring the car in today. Besides, I'm busy.

"Listen, Ed. Today I'm going to land Wildcat Casey behind the bars on a charge of burglary and assault. How's that? Yes I know who he is and all about him, and I've got the witnesses to prove my case."

A low whistle registered Cranweiler's astonishment and admiration.

"But I've got no time to bother with anything else today," Duvenney went on. "You tell them I'll drive out there tonight."

Fifteen minutes later a police machine came to a screeching halt in front of the apartment house where Theodore Burrell lived, and four detectives leaped out and ran up the steps.

"Who are you gentlemen looking for?" inquired the janitor, looking up from the brass rail he was polishing.

"Theodore Burrell," said the foremost of the detectives.

"He just this minute gone out," volunteered the custodian.

Chapter 10

Three Cars

A few hours after the supposed Theodore Burrell had "vanished," Casey, garbed in the greasy overalls and jumper of an automobile mechanic, and carrying a tool kit, turned in at the gate of Duvenney's residence. He walked right up to the front door, and appeared to press the bell button.

As a matter of fact, however, this was but a bit of acting to deceive anybody who might be at the window of one of the several houses across the street. In reality he pressed his finger against the stone beside the button.

He waited with an air of patient unconcern, whistling as he turned to glance casually around the grounds. Then, when nobody answered the supposed ring, he placed his finger on the button and pushed.

Apparently making up his mind that he would have better luck at the back door, he did not wait for the housekeeper, the solitary occupant of the house at that hour of the day, to arrive at the front, but sauntered around the side of the house.

By the time the puzzled woman had looked up and down the street a few times, he was safely hidden in the garage, the door to which he fortunately had found unlocked. Had it been locked it was his intention to speak to the housekeeper and tell her he had been sent by the lawyer to repair his machine, taking the chance that she might mention it to Duvenney that evening and so arouse his suspicions.

Making sure that he could not be observed from the house through the windows of the garage, he threw up the hood of the car and set to work with a small drill.

"It is a shame," he muttered to himself, "to butcher a splendid car this way. But still it won't be much of a job to braze in a little patch—if the old bus isn't left here to rust while her owner serves his stretch in the pen."

Placing the pointed part of the drill against the waterjacket, he carefully cut through the tough steel until a tiny stream of water spurted out. Then he drained the radiator, plugged the hold with a little piece of wax, smeared a bit of black grease over it, and refilled the radiator.

The door of the garage leading to the rear street, he found, operated on a snap lock, and could be opened without a key from the inside. Shouldering his tools again, he stepped forth, closed the door behind him, lighted a cigarette, and strolled off.

At that same moment Edna Raalhof was facing Scott Duvenney, in the latter's office.

"I don't know what else I can do to convince you of my good faith, Edna," he was saying. I am simply going out to see these men tonight to tip them off to a little job which can be pulled down in the lower end of the city."

And in a manner oddly in contrast with his former domineering attitude toward her, he proceeded to sketch the outlines of a plan for the robbery of an automobile agency.

"You see," he said, "they have seven new cars in stock. From this girl of Cranweiler's we planted in their office, we got the keys to the locks on those cars and had them duplicated. No one knows the keys have ever been out of the place. They'll break in Saturday night. Before Sunday morning each one of those cars will have had its numbers and secret identification marks changed, and will be on its way into a different state with a fake bill of sale in the hands of the driver. By the time the robbery is discovered, Monday morning, they will have had more than twenty-four hours start, and you know a machine can travel a long distance in twenty-four hours steady running."

Edna sat studying him, her elbow on her crossed knee, and her chin resting in her cupped hand.

"And this is the only job you have on hand at present, Scott?" she said.

"Yes," he replied.

"And there are no proceeds of former operations yet undivided?" she asked sharply.

"No," he said, but she did not fail to note the faint flicker of uneasiness in his eye.

"I warn you, Scott," she said as she rose, "you can't double-cross me, and it will be better for you if you don't try."

A look of crafty venom took the place of his assumed sincerity when the door had closed behind her, and for several moments he gave way to subdued profanity.

"Now why couldn't that—" he caught himself in the act of calling her a vile name. "Now why couldn't that girl," he repeated, "have taken the homage I was ready to give her. She could have had everything else in the world I could give her. But the little spitfire has the arrogance to turn me down and give me orders in the same breath. And she thinks she's going to walk off with the lion's share!" Again he gave way to profanity, which was interrupted by the telephone bell.

"Hello, that you, Mr. Duvenney?" came the voice over the wire. "This is Gravers, of headquarters. I've just been out hunting up this fellow Burrell. The chief told me to report to you."

"Did you get him?" inquired the lawyer eagerly.

"Naw. He'd beat it by the time we got up to his place, and from the looks of things around there I'd say he ain't coming back. One thing's got me stopped though. Can't dope it out. We tried to phone headquarters soon as we found this bird had flew away, but his wire was dead. Then I found out why. He'd cut it. Got any idea why he should cut his own telephone wire before beating it?"

"No-o," said Duvenney slowly, his mind busy trying to grasp the import of the supposed Burrell's disappearance.

"It's a foolish thing to mention," explained the detective. "Such a funny thing for a guy to do I was wondering if it mightn't mean something."

"No," said the lawyer, "I can't think of any reason. You fellows are going to keep after him aren't you?"

"Oh sure," Gravers said, "We're sticking on the job. Got a good description of him. We'll pick him up before long."

"You will like the devil," muttered Duvenney as he hung up the receiver. "Any man that can beat up Solly Wertheimer and Greasy Gorman, give a description of an automobile from the tracks it leaves in the road, and get away from that little spitfire and her father, is too much for a bunch of flatfooted boneheads like Gravers."

Duvenney began to get distinctly worried. For the second time within twenty-four hours he experienced the sensation of startled fear, an emotion to which he had long previously been a stranger. He even caught himself contemplating sudden flight. Caught between two fires, threatened on one side by a mere slip of a girl whom deep in his consciousness he recognized as too clever for him, and on the other by this secret investigator whose methods were so unusual and disconcerting, he felt the menace of unseen powers closing in around him.

Cowardice, however, was not among the lawyer's many vices, and with an effort of his will he pulled himself together, and began desperately to plan his defenses.

So far as Casey was concerned, he would have to be more careful in his dealings with members of the gang. He would have to disappear from active participation in its affairs, dealing only through Cranweiler. Then if Cranweiler "squealed" it would be only the word of a disgruntled employee against a powerful and influential employer. And he would be sure that there were no witnesses to his talks with Cranweiler.

This once, tonight, he would go out to the Willis farm for his share of the spoils. But in the future he would not even appear as counsel for any of the boys who fell into the coils of the police, but handle their cases through another lawyer.

So far as Edna was concerned—well, he guessed it would be better to play square with her after all until after all danger from Wildcat Casey's investigation was past. Then he would attend to her, "good and proper," he told himself. The situation might not be so bad after all.

Thus encouraging himself, he turned to scan his afternoon paper. In it he read of the conviction of Greasy Gorman and Solly Wertheimer. Robbed of his protecting influence, and defended by an inexperienced young lawyer with more ideals than tricks in his legal equipment, the men had been "railroaded" through the court.

Remembering his suspicion that they were making bootlegger profits which they were not sharing with him, the suspicion upon which he had abandoned them to their fate, he sat up suddenly in his chair.

Who but Burrell, whom he now knew to be Casey, was responsible for this suspicion. Again he swore. So that was it. Casey had deliberately sewn that little seed of suspicion, and had achieved his purpose in doing it.

This Casey, he reflected, setting his jaw in determination, was too clever a person to take any chances with. He would not give up his trip that night to the Willis farm, but he would go "heeled." With deliberation he opened a drawer of his desk and took therefrom a heavy automatic, and slipped it into his pocket.

As he slipped away from the city that evening, it was natural, considering this frame of mind, that he glanced frequently over his shoulder to see if any other machine was following him.

And there was. Though it was so far in back that it might well have escaped his attention in the gathering dusk. It was a full eighth of a mile behind, but it seemed to be keeping pace with him. Coming to the end of a badly paved stretch of road, he determined to test his suspicions, and stepped on the accelerator, his car shooting ahead smoothly and powerfully. If the car behind also speeded up while still on the bad road he would know for certain.

It did.

Then he slowed down. The other car did likewise.

As he slid gently down an incline and noted the long steep grade ahead a plan came to him. At the bottom he shifted into second gear and crept up the incline. Half way up the hill he turned in his seat for a careful look. The plan was working. The other car was making no attempt to close up on him, but apparently had also shifted into second. Even if it had not, he observed, it was taking the grade so slowly that it would not be able to pick up well until it had topped the grade.

On passing the top himself, he shifted back into high and opened the throttle wide, taking the next down grade with a roaring rush which had carried him out of sight before the second car came over the brow.

The driver of the latter, finally sensing what had happened, put on frantic speed also, but when five minutes' desperate driving failed to bring the taillight of the lawyer's car into view, gave up the chase, turned reluctantly and headed back toward the city.

It was then that a third car came by, the long beam of its

spotlight focused on the center of he road, traveling swiftly and silently, with no sound but the sucking rush of air in the carburetor and the faint moan of a perfectly muffled exhaust.

The driver of the second car gasped, again swung around, narrowly escaping the ditch, and followed it.

Chapter 11

The End of the Trail

Duvenney's motor had begun to knock, and was running with disconcerting unevenness as he turned off the main road at the entrance to a prosperous looking farm, congratulating himself upon his escape from the pursuing car.

The house was some distance from the road, and with its lights switched off he was confident his car could not be seen. By the time he finished his conference with Shorty Granville and Elmer Cady, the two crooks he had come out there to meet, he figured that there would be little chance that his pursuer would be in the vicinity, and he could then with greater safety inspect the engine.

"Hello, Willis," he said to the flannel-shirted owner of the property, who opened the door. "Are Granville and Cady here?"

"Yep," responded the other. "Come before dark. Told 'em to put their car around back. Not that anybody'd think it strange to see a machine standing here—still, it's better to be safe. Come on in."

"Everything clear?" asked the lawyer, shedding his overcoat.

"Yep. Sent the Missus and the girl off to the movies in the

flivver. You got a full hour and a half to chin. If yeh don't want me f'r anything right away I'm going down to feed the cows."

Duvenney nodded his assent and stepped into the room where the two crooks were waiting for him.

Humming a little tune, the farmer strolled out into the kitchen, and leisurely changed from his slippers to a pair of heavy shoes. Then he took down a lantern from a shelf over the sink and lighted it. When it was burning to his satisfaction he threw open the door and stepped out into the night, still humming.

His tune ended in an inarticulate grunt as a blackjack in the hands of a muscular young man descended upon his skull.

Three forms bent quickly over him. One of them was Wildcat Casey.

"It was the only safe way," the detective whispered to his companions. "You fellows didn't see this, of course. Now take him down to the barn and tie him up. You're sure to find some rope down there. Then come back here with Mr. Durwent."

In less than four minutes they were back, all four of them slipping noiselessly into the house.

In the living room Duvenney and the two crooks had gotten quickly to business, which was arriving at an agreement as to the exact division of the proceeds of a "job" which the two had "pulled" a week or so before.

Granville and Cady were not the sort of men who betrayed their status either in face, bearing or general appearance. It would have taken a keen reader of character to understand the significance of the slight evasiveness in their eyes at times, and the hair-trigger nerves beneath their easy poses. To the casual observer they might have been a pair of wide awake salesmen, perhaps a trifle overly inclined to fastidiousness of dress. But they were marked men. Both had serious police records, and Duvenney deemed it safer to meet them in secret rather than have them call at his office.

The loot, it had been previously agreed, was to be divided three ways. But Duvenney was objecting to their claim for certain expenses as exorbitant. Finally, however, a compromise was effected, and the money changed hands.

"I want you boys to lie low for a couple of weeks," Duvenney was saying, "because—What the devil's the matter with you, Shorty?"

With an oath the man addressed whirled in his chair, in a single rapid movement drawing an automatic from the holster beneath his coat and firing into the darkness of the hallway.

"Quick!" he yelled, "Beat it! The bulls!"

At the same instant Cady, who also had pulled his gun and was crouching behind the table, fired.

There followed the deafening crash of a fusillade in a confined space. Duvenney stood, mouth agape, extending his hands in a futile, protective movement. Granville raised his arm to sweep the oil lamp from the table, but a bullet paralyzed it before he could accomplish his purpose, and his gun dropped from his nerveless fingers. At the same instant Cady howled and collapsed, a bullet in his thigh.

The instant of silence which followed seemed an eternity.

Then a figure in the jumper and overalls of an automobile mechanic stepped from the darkness of the hall into the room, followed by two eager looking youngsters and a middle aged man.

"C-Casey!" stammered the lawyer.

"Correct," admitted that individual. "I guess we've got the goods on you, old man—Keep away from that gun, Shorty —How's that leg of yours Cady; didn't break the bone I hope—Too quick with your gun play—I didn't get you anything, you see.

"Here, you fellows pick up those gats while I put the nippers on this trio," he continued, turning to the younger men.

"What's the meaning of this outrage?" blustered Duvenney, at last getting a grip on himself. "You sneaking spy! I'll put you behind—"

"Calm yourself, Duvenney. Calm yourself," Casey advised. "We've got you dead to rights this time. We overheard all your conversation, and saw the money passed. All your money, pull and knowledge of the law won't get you off this time. Allow me to introduce the company.

"This gentleman," indicating one of the younger men, "is Mr. O'Reilley, of *The Star*. And this is Mr. Kent of *The Blade*. Their papers are going to have a whale of a first-page yarn in the morning. 'PROMINENT LAWYER ARRESTED AS HEAD OF AUTO-BANDIT GANG' and all that sort of thing. I don't think your friends on the police force will be able to help you much unless they undertake to suppress evidence by murdering O'Reilley and Kent, and Mr. Durwent here—You know Mr. Durwent, at least by reputation, I assume. As one of the leaders of the Civic League I think his testimony would overbalance yours in the eyes of a jury. Oh no, Duvenney, don't delude yourself with any false hopes."

The lawyer made no further attempt to bluff out the situation, but slumped into a chair, a picture of dejection.

"Now, Mr. Casey, what is our next move?" asked Durwent, palpably nervous from the excitement.

"I should say the best thing would be for you and Kent and O'Reilley to take my car and go for a warrant and a regular police officer, while I stay here on guard."

"Say," asked O'Reilley, as the three were leaving, "I've been trying all along to puzzle out how you trailed this bird out here tonight. I didn't catch sight of his tail lamp the whole way out. Yet you told us you were trailing him and didn't know where he was going. What's the answer?"

Casey grinned.

"He left a water trail," he explained. "This afternoon I bored a small hole in the waterjacket of his motor and plugged it with wax. The instant the motor heated up the wax melted, and the water began to spill. I picked up the trail at his garage and just followed it. That's all. We weren't more than five minutes behind him, and the water didn't have time to evaporate. I didn't want him to know he was being followed. I thought I'd lost him once though. Another car with a leaky radiator must have passed over the road somewhere ahead of him for a stretch. But it was leaking so badly that when we got to where it turned off the road I knew which was which."

"Some sleuthing, I'll say," remarked O'Reilley admiringly as he followed the others to the door.

When they had gone, Casey made sure that his prisoners were secure, and sat down to wait.

"There's one thing I'll get you for though, Casey," said Duvenney, looking up after a bit. "I'll see that you're jailed for your attack on Miss Raalhof and her father. That was a dirty piece of work, Casey, and your position as a detective won't relieve you of responsibility for it."

"You're raving," said Casey curtly. "In the first place, after what I saw through the window of your attack on her, you're in no position to make such an accusation. In the second place, as you very well know, or easily can convince yourself, Edna Raalhof and her father attacked me. And in the third place, you won't bring about my arrest, because by the time Durwent returns with a warrant and an officer to serve it on you I will be gone.

"But while we're on the subject of Edna Raalhof, suppose you come clean, and tell me how deeply she's in this thing."

"Edna will speak for herself," interrupted a feminine voice from the door. And the girl, looking very slim in her neat masculine attire, sauntered easily into the room, a sardonic little smile pulling down the corners of her mouth.

In her hand she held a revolver, and it was pointed steadily at Casey. For a moment the pair looked at each other. Then reluctantly, though without waiting for the command, Casey elevated his hands above his head. There was a recklessness in her manner and a determination in her glance that told him this time she would not hesitate to shoot, and that he could not repeat his strategy of the night before in disarming her.

"Well?" he asked finally.

"Back up to that wall," she commanded.

He complied.

"I'm going to take your gun away from you," she said, advancing confidently. "If you make a move—if you so much as lower your arm an inch, I'll drill you."

Placing the muzzle of her gun against his stomach, she thrust her other hand inside his coat, fumbling for his weapon.

Gently Casey shifted his weight to one foot, and apparently without making a motion, tapped his heel twice against the base of the wall. Instinctively Edna's glance dropped, seeking the cause of the sound. In that same instant Casey's arm described a swift circle downward, brushing her weapon to one side. Too late by a split second the gun barked, driving its bullet into the wall.

Then he had her firmly by the wrists, holding the hand that grasped the revolver carefully away from him. She struggled convulsively.

"Drop the gun," he ordered. "I don't want to hurt you."

A twist of her wrist would have made her drop it. But he could not bring himself to inflict this pain on her; so he held her calmly until her rage should wear itself out.

Finally she relaxed, her fingers opened and the gun clattered to the floor.

"You win," she said bitterly, staggering back as he released her wrists, and looking up at him with the expression of a hurt child. "I shall go now. I suppose you have no charge against me."

"No," he admitted slowly. "I have no evidence against you—yet."

Half way to the door she stopped short. The telephone was ringing, and she caught a gleam in Duvenney's eye. She turned quickly.

"That's probably Cranweiler," she said to Casey. "If you answer it, you'll scare him off. Let me."

Casey hesitated in astonishment. Her change of front had been to quick for him.

"I'll play square," she pleaded. "I won't give you away. Besides, you can't answer it yourself without doing so anyway."

At his nod of assent, she ran across the room and lifted the receiver from the hook. Casey followed, standing close beside her and insisting by his motions that she hold the receiver so he also could hear what was being said.

"This is Miss Raalhof speaking," she said quickly. "Mr. Duvenney isn't here, but he said if you called I was to take your message."

"Tell him the boys pulled that deal we were talking about," said Cranweiler. "It's a cool seventy-five thousand. They're taking it up to Martin's now." And he hung up.

The words seemed to galvanize the girl. With all her young strength, she gave Casey a push, as he, caught off his balance, stumbled and fell.

The next instant she had sent the lamp crashing to the floor and had gone.

Chapter 12

The Heart of a Woman

When Duvenney had told Edna, earlier in the day at his office, that his only purpose in seeing Shorty Granville and Elmer Cady that night was to give them their instructions in the robbery of the automobile salesrooms for which he had arranged, and had assured her that his organization had no other definite enterprise underway, she knew he was lying.

Only the day before, she had by clever questioning gotten a pretty good idea from Cranweiler of the recent activities of Granville and Cady, as well as a hint of the project to rob Mike Minnot, the wealthy bootlegger, who, as Duvenney had found out, would be returning to the city that night with some $75,000 in cash, the proceeds from a sale of a supposed fishing schooner.

Edna had not been able to find out from Cranweiler just where Minnot was to be held up, so she had a double purpose that night in following Duvenney. One was to confront him most effectively with the futility of his lie to her, and the other was to force him to split with her the money stolen from Minnot.

But Duvenney had outwitted her with his tactics on the hill, and she had finally given up the chase and turned back to the city. By a lucky chance her keen eyes recognized Casey in the person of the smudgy auto mechanic at the wheel of the next car which came along in the same direction that Duvenney had taken, and she had found her way to Duvenney by following Casey.

She had witnessed the attack on Willis when he stepped out the back door of the farmhouse, and cautiously had followed Casey and his party inside.

Her inspiration came in a flash when Cranweiler mentioned that the bandits were taking their loot "up to Martin's." This meant, she knew, the apartment of Jake Martin, a member of Duvenney's ring, in a fashionable suburb in the northern section.

When she shoved Casey aside, upset the lamp, and slipped from the room in the confusion, she knew she had a sporting chance of arriving at Martin's place before the bandits did.

Her plan, formulated as she ran to her machine, was a bold one.

Throwing caution to the winds, she raced at full speed toward this neighborhood, and arriving there, drew up at the curb a few feet beyond the apartment house entrance, her machine facing in the opposite direction from that which she expected the bandit car to come. She sat there waiting, tense under the nervous strain, holding her automatic hidden from glance of any casual passer-by.

Once, as a machine stopped in front of the building, she was half way out of her own car before she discovered its occupants were not the ones for whom she was looking.

Then they came.

Swinging in to the curb just behind her own, the bandit machine, an innocent enough looking car, pulled up. Two men climbed out, then a third, who carried a large bundle wrapped in newspaper.

Edna slipped out of her own machine at the same instant as the man with the bundle straightened up. For the moment the sidewalk was deserted at this spot, and all the figures stood out clearly in the glare of the electric light.

When the man with the bundle looked up, he gazed straight into the muzzle of her automatic.

"Hands up, all three of you!" she commanded sharply. "I'll plug the first one of you that makes the slightest move to draw his gun."

The last thing in the world that three automobile bandits look for is to be themselves held up by a single slim youth. The two bandits who had stepped out of the machine first, had glanced sharply up and down the street, despite their careless manner, but they were looking for blue uniforms, and paid not the slightest attention to the single supposed stripling in the other car.

Taken completely by surprise, they responded instantly to Edna's galvanizing command. Nor did any of them care to take a chance on reaching for his own gun after one glance into her eyes. They were momentarily dazed by the sudden turn in the situation.

"Toss that bundle into my car," she continued, and as the man complied with evident reluctance, "Now, about face, all of you. Keep your hands straight up above your heads, and walk up the street to the corner. The first man that stops, lowers his hands or turns his head I'll drill through his heart—and I can do it too. Make it snappy, now!"

As the three started off abreast, the girl drew a deep breath, and risking no longer wait, leaped lightly into her machine, and with a roar shot away from the curb.

By this time several people were running up the street from the direction in which she had sent the bandits, two men ran out of the apartment house, and a police whistle sounded about a block away.

As her machine leaped away like a living thing Edna figured, and rightly, that the bandits would not dare shoot, since they could not themselves stand an interview with the police, but would concern themselves immediately with their own escape.

Twisting and turning through the streets of the suburb, she heard the clamor of the pursuit die away behind her.

Now she faced the real problem into which her bold action had led her, that of communicating with her father, and finding a hiding place until Wildcat Casey should give up the chase.

Had Edna been an amateur in crime she would have planned an escape from the city. She knew, however, that there is no safer hiding place than a big city, where most people know little of their neighbors and care less.

She could find a temporary haven in the little apartment which she and her father had leased for the year before they moved to the country. They had not occupied it for some time, but she still had her key, and, she remembered, there was some old clothing of hers there with which she might make shift to disguise herself.

Dared she risk it?

She decided she would, for just long enough to get rid of her telltale masculine attire and to telephone her father to come in and meet her. She was quite sure she had never mentioned the apartment at the country club, and had never spoken of it to Duvenney. There was not much chance, therefore, that Casey knew of its existence or would find it before the pair of them were ready to disappear into the slums somewhere.

About four squares from the place, she abandoned her machine, and walked the rest of the way with the newspaper bundle under her arm. Once she got a scare. A pedestrian whom she had to pass in the full glare of an arc light glanced curiously at her, and evidently suspecting her sex from her delicate features and the manner in which her cap was pulled down all the way over her hair, halted and turned to stare, then evidently thought better of it and went on about his business.

Once in the apartment, she telephone immediately to her father, then proceeded to change her attire.

From an old trunk she took a mussed skirt and an old sweater. She was lucky too, in finding a curling iron, with which she transformed the normal wave of her bobbed tresses into a mop of frizzed hair.

She surveyed herself with satisfaction. Then upon sudden thought she added a finishing touch in the shape of a pair of shell rimmed spectacles of her father. It hurt her eyes to look through them, but this, she thought would serve to help along the disguise by changing their expression somewhat.

With no little nervous impatience she now awaited her father's arrival. She had told him to do everything possible to change his appearance before he left, so they would be ready to leave on the instant.

Edna was developing an uneasy fear of Casey's abilities, and would not feel settled until she was safely away from the place. The man was uncannily swift and direct in his movements.

At a slight tap on the door she leaped from her chair, as though the sound had touched a raw nerve.

"Are you there, Edna?" came the subdued voice of Sigmund Raalhof.

She ran to the door and threw it open.

"Quick," she said, pulling him inside and dragging him to the light, the better to inspect his appearance. "Let me see how you look, then we must be going. Good! That threadbare suit, that ragged droop instead of the waxed ends of your moustache is fine. Wait, you need a dirty neck and collar, and a bit of grime rubbed into your face and hands. And, here, get rid of your glasses."

She ran to a corner of the room, where she rubbed her hands on the dusty floor; then with a few quick manipulations produced the effect she desired in him.

"Where is the money?" he asked.

"Here," she said, thrusting the newspaper bundle into his hand. "Now we must go. Casey is a quick worker, and—"

"Don't go just yet," came a third voice from the doorway. At the sound of it Edna stiffened. Slowly she turned.

Casey had stepped into the room and closed the door softly behind him. He held his revolver carelessly, but both father and daughter knew that it was ready for instant action.

"First of all, Mr. Raalhof," he said, "I'll thank you to lay that valuable little bundle on the table. Now just reach into your pocket and take out your gun very carefully and lay it on the table also—and if you think you can shoot quicker than I can, just go ahead and take the chance."

But Raalhof was no gunman. He quietly put his weapon where Casey told him to, at the same time flashing a questioning glance toward Edna.

"And will you surrender yours too?" he asked.

"No!" she flared. Inside the pocket of her dress her little hand spasmodically clutched the handle of her automatic.

Casey took a step toward her.

"Yes," she said, and flung it clattering to the floor at his feet. Tears of vexation welled up in her eyes. She knew she could not shoot him, and she knew he knew she couldn't. Then pride drove away the tears. She drew herself up, and looked at him coldly, and turned her back to him. And in that fleeting instant she managed, by a meaning glance and a little gesture concealed from Casey, to convey a message to her father.

She turned quickly, challenging the detective's glance.

"Well," she demanded sarcastically, "hadn't you better put the bracelets on me for safekeeping?"

At this instant, Raalhof measured the distance between

himself and the door to the room beyond, and leaped for it. Edna's ruse worked. Casey did not shoot. Instead he leaped after him, and as he disappeared through the door there came the sounds of a vicious struggle.

Edna did not bother to pick up one of the guns. She knew she would not bring herself to use it on this man. Instead of rescuing her father, she must heartlessly leave him to his fate. Nor, strangely enough, did this worry her.

She seized the bundle of currency and started for the door. Half way across the room, she paused suddenly, glancing back toward the room whence came the thud of fists and the grunts of the struggling men, then dropping her eyes to the package of currency in her hand.

For an instant, she stood. Then with a flash of something like exaltation in her eyes, she tossed the bundle back on the table, softly opened the door, as softly closed it behind her, and slipped out into the dawn of a new day.

THE END

Breinigsville, PA USA
07 April 2010
235676BV00001B/22/A